Tease Me

Also From J. Kenner

Stark Security
Shattered With You
Broken With You
Ruined With You

The Stark Saga:
Release Me
Claim Me
Complete Me
Anchor Me
Lost With Me
Damien

Stark Ever After:
Take Me
Have Me
Play My Game
Seduce Me
Unwrap Me
Deepest Kiss
Entice Me
Hold Me
Please Me
Indulge Me
Delight Me

Stark International
Steele Trilogy:
Say My Name
On My Knees
Under My Skin
Take My Dare (novella, includes bonus short story: Steal My Heart)

Stark World Standalone Stories:
Justify Me (part of the Lexi Blake Crossover Collection)

Jamie & Ryan Novellas:
Tame Me
Tempt Me

Dallas & Jane (S.I.N. Trilogy):
Dirtiest Secret
Hottest Mess
Sweetest Taboo

Most Wanted:
Wanted
Heated
Ignited

Wicked Nights:
Wicked Grind
Wicked Dirty
Wicked Torture

Man of the Month:
Down On Me
Hold On Tight
Need You Now
Start Me Up
Get It On
In Your Eyes
Turn Me On
Shake It Up
All Night Long
In Too Deep
Light My Fire
Walk The Line
Bar Bites: A Man of the Month Cookbook

Tease Me

A Stark International Security Novel

By J. Kenner

Tease Me
A Stark International Security Novel
By J. Kenner

Copyright 2020 Julie Kenner
ISBN: 978-1-951812-09-6

Published by Blue Box Press, an imprint of Evil Eye Concepts, Incorporated

Acknowledgments from the Author

To the J. Kenner Krew, my awesome Facebook reader group, to all my newsletter subscribers, and to Liz Berry for suggesting that I turn much shorter bonus content into this full novel!

This story started out as bonus content in my newsletter, with a chapter appearing every month in its raw, unedited, straight-from-my-computer-with-no-plan form. Readers and I had such fun with the story that I ended up cleaning it up and significantly expanding it into this book for 1001 Dark Nights after chatting with Liz about it at a conference last year.

So thanks to all of you! And I'm onto another story in my newsletter now! Subscribe so that you don't miss a thing!

Join JK's Facebook group!
https://www.facebook.com/groups/jkenner/

Subscribe to JK's Newsletter

Acknowledgements

[faded, illegible text]

Sign up for the 1001 Dark Nights Newsletter
and be entered to win a Tiffany Lock necklace.

There's a contest every quarter!

Go to www.1001DarkNights.com to subscribe.

As a bonus, all subscribers can download
FIVE FREE exclusive books!

Prologue

Ryan Hunter watched the young woman he'd been hired to protect absently spin the gold ring on her finger. He doubted she even realized what she was doing. Instead, she was absorbed by the view outside the train's window. The moonlit sand. The craggy mountains beyond. And the danger hiding in the moon-cast shadows.

"Felicia."

She jumped, then turned to face him, her brown eyes bloodshot and puffy. An apologetic smile touched her lips as she pushed a lock of midnight-black hair off of her face, the dark curl in contrast to her pale skin, paler now that all of her makeup had sloughed off during their escape.

She seemed to look right through him, and he imagined she was looking back at the bomb-shattered buildings. The bodies scattered in the streets. They might be miles away now, but he was certain she could still see them. God knew he could.

With a sigh, she turned back to the window. "It looks so peaceful," she said, her soft British accent contrasting with the hard reality that surrounded them. "I can barely wrap my head around the reality that there's a coup going on. An actual coup. And that we're right in the middle of it." She bit her lower lip, then pulled the shade down, obscuring the view.

For a moment, she simply sat there, staring at the now-blocked window. Then she turned to face him, her expressionless eyes meeting his as she asked, very simply, "Are we going to get out of this alive?" She looked calm. As if the world of military coups and midnight escapes was old hat to her. Only the slight quiver in her voice gave away her simmering terror.

He took her hands, planning to spew all the platitudes that he knew she wanted to hear. Of course they were going to get out. Of course they would be just fine. That was why her father had hired a security firm. That's why the firm had sent Ryan. That's why they were moving quickly and carefully.

But he didn't say any of that. She deserved the truth. More than that, she was smart enough to already know it. "We're damn well going to try."

For a moment, she just held tight to him, as if he truly had the power to ensure her safety. Then she pulled her hands free, crossed her arms over her chest, and tucked her hands into her armpits as she hugged herself tight. Her thin shoulders rose and fell, and she nodded slowly, as if absorbing his words. "I hate myself for being so stupid."

"You aren't stupid."

She cocked her head, looking ridiculously young. "I followed a man I barely knew to an unstable country in the Middle East. A country I'm not even sure existed a month ago, and I'm pretty sure won't exist next week. If it's even still a country right now, and not just a bombed-out hole in the ground."

Ryan bit back a grimace. She wasn't wrong. They were deep inside disputed territory, peaceful only days ago, but now a hotbed of militant activity. And, yes, all the signs that the region was unstable had been there from the moment that Felicia had left London. One glance at a newspaper or one search on the Internet would have revealed the nature of the conflict and the danger of traveling to this part of the globe. Maybe she'd still have come and maybe she wouldn't have, but there would have been no denying the red flags.

But she'd done none of that. She'd met a man and fallen hard. She'd wanted him, and Felicia Cartwright was used to getting what she wanted.

So when Mikal Safar had invited her back to meet his wealthy and politically powerful family, she'd gone without hesitation. But never once did she expect that dissidents would rise up. And she certainly never anticipated that they would murder Mikal and his father, thus inciting a rebellion that threatened the life of everyone with any sort of connection to Mikal's father or the other government leaders.

In fairness, after reading the pre-mission dossier, Ryan understood how Felicia had gotten herself mixed up in the mess. Felicia had grown up like a princess herself, her royal blood of the kind that was bestowed by generations of wealth, not birth. Her mother had died in childbirth, and Randall Cartwright had doted on his little girl, showering her with love, affection, and as many toys and luxuries as the London-based millionaire could afford. Which, as far as Ryan could tell, meant all of them.

Felicia was completely spoiled, used to getting her own way, and stubborn as hell. But despite all that, Ryan liked her. The girl had spunk, that was for sure. And she was an intriguing mixture of hard edges and soft personality. Like cotton candy encased in steel.

As if to prove the point, she cocked her head, staring him down. "See? You know I'm right. You're just afraid that if you admit that I'm an idiot, Daddy won't pay your fee."

He chuckled, her self-deprecating comment settling them both. "Your father knows you're not an idiot. But he also knows you are impulsive. And sometimes that looks like the same thing."

"Either way, we get to the same point. I shouldn't be here. I shouldn't have followed Mikal. And the day he disappeared, I should have headed straight for the border. Thank goodness the old lady—"

She broke off, choking back a sob. One of the servants in the Safar household had warned her that Mikal's disappearance wasn't because he'd been trying to escape before the coup—rudely not taking her with him—but that he'd been captured and beheaded. And then, with Felicia still reeling with shock, she'd warned the girl to do whatever she could to escape before she was also killed by the dissidents—or worse.

Ryan leaned forward, then used a finger to lift her chin, making a point to meet her chocolate brown eyes straight on. "You made an impulsive decision to follow a man you cared about, that's true. But it's also an age-old story. Don't beat yourself up for underestimating what you were getting yourself into. This isn't your world. You had no point of reference. And even if you'd paid attention and knew that the area was unstable, you trusted Mikal."

She sniffled and nodded. "I did. I know I probably shouldn't have—not after only knowing him such a short time—but I really and truly did."

"And from what I know of him, he was an upstanding man. Look at me," he demanded when she cast her eyes down. "You were sharp enough to trust that woman, and you called for help immediately. You didn't cry or hesitate. Despite your grief, you acted."

She rolled her eyes. "I did what I always do. I called my daddy. And he called you. So much for bravery."

"Don't you dare denigrate your actions. It wasn't as easy as pushing speed dial, and we both know it." The rebels had shut down cellular service, and she'd had to sneak into an occupied office building to find an outgoing landline. It had been that single act of cunning and bravery that made Ryan certain that she could handle whatever they would face during this escape.

Unfortunately, not breaking down into tears and self-pity wasn't the same thing as surviving. And as Mikal's guest, she was on the dissidents' radar. That made this whole thing a much more dangerous ordeal.

He drew a breath. "You're smart. You're resourceful. And you did the right thing. Don't go soft on me now."

"I'm sorry, you know."

"About what?"

She rolled her eyes. "All of this. It's my fault that you're stuck in the middle of the danger with me."

"Well, that's my job. I think we can give you a pass on that, okay?"

Her smile quivered a bit, but she nodded. She had a thin blanket, and she pulled it up over her stained white blouse.

"Try to get some sleep," he said. "We both need it, and so long as the train's moving, we're safe."

"Okay," she said, her heavy lids already drooping. A few moments later, her breathing became even, and he knew that she'd drifted off despite her fears. Not surprising. They'd been on the run for three days, working their way desperately toward the river—and the border that ran right down the middle of those deep, churning waters.

All they had to do was make it over the bridge and past the checkpoint, and they'd be home free.

The checkpoint.

That was going to be the tricky part. But hopefully it would go seamlessly. It had to, as he had no one he could call on for backup. Not now. He was on his own until he crossed that line. No allies, no resources. But once they were past the checkpoint, he could radio for support. He'd have air transport, backup.

He'd have the means to get her safe and home.

Three hundred miles.

They'd come so far already. Surely, he could take her that much further.

He leaned back, closed his eyes, and let the rumble of the train against his back soothe him into sleep.

* * * *

"What's happening?"

"We're slowing. I'm not sure why." His tense words seemed to underscore the *cha-cha-chunk* of the train, a harsh reminder that although they were moving, their destination remained elusive.

He'd awakened before Felicia, as soon as the rhythm of the wheels on the track had slowed. He'd sat quietly, studying the gray landscape, growing darker as the moon set behind the distant mountains. Now he turned his attention to her, forcing a smile in the hopes of keeping her calm as the hours wore on. He took her hand, his thumb brushing the gold ring on her finger. "It's okay. I'll take care of you."

Even in the dim light, he could see the blush rise up her neck to settle on her cheeks. She pressed her lips together, then nodded. "Ryan," she said, then cleared her throat. "Do you think it's us? Do they know we're on board?"

"I don't know. I hope not. Most likely we're approaching the river." If so, then the reduced speed made sense. If not…well, that very well could mean danger.

He glanced out the window again but couldn't see far enough. Then the track curved, and he breathed more easily, relief flowing through him like the water ahead. "It is the river. I can see the bridge up ahead."

Her smile lit her face, temporarily erasing the now-familiar lines of worry that hadn't faded even when she slept. "So we're still safe. And it's almost over."

"Almost," he confirmed. "But not yet." He leaned forward, taking her hands in his. "We can't get sloppy now. Tell me. Just like you'll tell them when we reach the checkpoint."

She squared her shoulders. "My name is Felicia Cartwright Hunter. I work for my father's company, and I came here to discuss a joint business venture with Mikal Safar. There were rumors that we were involved, but that was ridiculous."

She gave an imperious sniff, as if in disdain. "I have no interest in the political climate here, and certainly none in Mr. Safar. If I had, why would I have brought my fiancé with me, much less married him when we saw how lovely the setting was on the coastline?"

She leaned back, releasing his hands and studying him. "Was that okay?"

"Perfect." He only hoped it worked. Foreigners who had entered the country for recreation were, for the most part, being ushered across the checkpoint to safety. The question was going to be whether or not their marriage passed muster. And that was why Ryan—a man who'd never expected to marry anyone—was now legally wed to a woman he barely knew. A woman he would consensually divorce once they were back in London.

He studied her, smiling despite the circumstances. She was pretty and terrified, and on their wedding night, they'd shared a room and a bed. Both because there was no way he'd leave her alone, but also because they had to feed the illusion. Spies were everywhere, and Felicia was definitely being watched.

She'd been terrified and sad, and he'd held her close, soothing her and promising he'd do whatever was necessary in order to get her out safely. But that wasn't the kind of comfort she'd wanted or needed. She'd curled against him, her curves as enticing as the warmth of her body under the thin gown she'd worn to bed. She'd taken his hand, then pressed it to her lower belly. And all she'd said was *please.*

That was all it took. He had no girlfriend, no one he saw regularly. But he wasn't a monk. Not by a long shot. He'd taken what she offered, giving back as much as he could, wanting her to feel safe. Hell, just wanting her to *feel.* They were both scared. Both uncertain. But at least in bed they could forget.

It had started slow and sweet, but by the end, her fingernails had dug into his flesh and he'd held her close as the orgasm ripped through her.

After, she'd snuggled against him, thanked him for marrying her, thanked him for protecting her, and thanked him for fucking her.

She'd fallen asleep then, and he'd lain there for at least an hour, looking down at the woman who was, for the time being, his wife. And, yes, he would take care of her in whatever way she needed. He'd sworn an oath, and he took that vow as seriously as his oath as a professional. He would protect her with his life if that's what it came to. And he would damn sure do whatever was necessary to get her safely out of this war-torn area.

"Will it work?" she asked now. Her eyes were wide and earnest. "Will they believe us? There were photographs of me and Mikal…"

"I don't know," he said honestly. "But it's the best chance we've got."

The corner of her mouth trembled, and she blinked as a single tear spilled down her cheek. "I'm okay. Promise. Just scared. And—well, no matter what, at least I can always say that my first husband was one hell of a good-looking man."

"And my first wife was the bravest woman I—*fuck!*"

The curse was ripped from him, the sound of it buried under Felicia's scream as a surreal orange light filled the rail car, along with the ear-splitting blast of a nearby bomb's detonation.

Ryan stood, then reached for Felicia, only to be slammed back into his seat when the train lurched forward as it picked up speed.

"We're going *toward* the bomb?" Fear laced her voice, her eyes reflecting her terror.

"We're almost to the bridge," he said, his voice tight. He'd flinched against the sun-bright blast, but when he'd opened his eyes, some light still lingered, and he saw that they were closer to the bridge than he'd realized. There was still a chance. Assuming they hadn't been boarded. Assuming the blast was an attempt to derail them—an attempt that had failed. "The crew wants over the border as much as we do. They'll try for the bridge."

"And get us killed."

He shook his head. "If we haven't been boarded, we might make it."

"Have we been?"

"I don't know. But the train never fully stopped. Hopefully that means we haven't been."

But that promising possibility was shot down—literally—by a spray of automatic weapon fire that riddled the ceiling. Ryan yanked her to the floor, covering her body with his. He was unarmed, having been searched three times before boarding the train. Smuggling a weapon hadn't been an option. He'd wished at the time that there'd been another way. He wished that even more fervently now as at least a dozen men in full combat garb rushed toward them.

"Move," the burliest of the group said, his English heavily accented.

Ryan shifted position and lifted his hands, revealing his own gold band. "Please don't harm my wife. We're newlyweds. We came here for a vacation mixed with some business. We're trying to get back home."

The man raised his rifle, then aimed it right at Ryan's chest. "Move," he repeated. "Or your blood will stain the woman before we kill her, too." A malicious smile slithered over his face. "But first we shall enjoy her, no?"

Ryan heard Felicia's whimper. It didn't take long to calculate his odds. All things considered, he had exactly zero in his favor. Without a choice, he nodded, hoping that the thug's superior would be more reasonable.

With Felicia walking on trembling legs in front of him, they were ushered through the next carriage. It was a freight car, with the sliding doors open. The night loomed beyond the car, and the river churned beneath them, dark and ominous, and altogether too far away for Ryan to be sure of survival.

Felicia stopped, her hand seeking his. He took it, knowing immediately what had made her halt. In front of them, he could see a cluster of passengers through the doors connecting their car to the next—and each and every person was writhing as bullets from unseen assailants riddled their bodies and they collapsed out of sight, dying ignobly on the hard, cold floor of the freighter.

"Mikal Safar," the burly man said from behind them as Ryan took a step closer to Felicia, the icy burn of his training warring with hot, liquid fear. "The girl is his," the man growled. "And he is scum."

The dissident's rifle pressed into Ryan's lower back, pushing him closer to Felicia. "We're jumping. Be ready." Ryan's whisper was little more than breath, and he hoped she'd heard and understood.

Another hard push of the barrel, powerful enough to bruise Ryan's spine, as the other men around him laughed and crowed. "And you, pig, are nothing but meat."

Ryan forced himself not to shudder as he gathered his strength, a split second of time seeming to pass like minutes. He hoped she understood the risk he was taking. Hoped she knew it was the only way. They probably wouldn't survive the fall, but at least they would have a chance. At least they would be choosing. If they stayed in the car, they'd be dead within minutes at these bastards' hands. Probably seconds.

He didn't count to three, just launched himself sideways, grabbing Felicia by the arm as he threw both of them toward the open doorway. At the same time, he twisted his body away from the gun, his muscles crying out in protest against a maneuver that even all of his training and hours in the gym couldn't have anticipated.

He felt the cool rush of air on his face as they neared the door, then the stabbing pain and liquid heat from the blood that poured out of his side. He'd moved enough to save his spine, but not to escape the bullet.

Still, if they could just get through that freight door…

The thought was still in his head as he felt the slam of the hard, hot surface of the carriage floor beneath him. And then the shooting pain of a metal-toed boot landing hard against his ribs before crushing down on his wrist, forcing him to release the death-grip on Felicia's arm.

She lay beside him, a bubble of blood on her mouth, her hands pressed to a gaping wound in her gut. Another wave of pain cut through him. Not physical this time. The pain of loss. The pain of knowing that he'd failed her.

"I'm sorry," she whispered, the word cracked and barely audible, but echoing his thoughts with perfect clarity. "Should… never… have… come."

He struggled, trying to move, the world growing dim around him, his arm screaming from the pain of the heavy boot holding him down. And then it was him screaming, too, his throat raw from the sound of his agonized protests as three of the men hauled Felicia to her feet, the wound gushing so much blood he knew she would never survive the injury. At that point, though, it didn't matter. Whether it was the wound or the river, he knew that she was dead. His mission. His responsibility.

His wife.

As the gray cloud of unconsciousness settled over him, he watched them push her off the train and into the dark, forbidding water of the river.

Chapter One

Many Years Later

"This is Jamie Archer," I say, after tapping the ear bud to connect the phone that's tucked away inside my purse on the far side of the room.

"Your professional name?" Even over the phone, I can hear the surprise in Nikki's voice. I understand why, too. After all, I'd told her what I had in mind for tonight, and there's not a shred of work on the agenda. "Does this mean you abandoned your plan?"

I hear the hope and bite back a frown as I shimmy into the red silk dress I've bought for this evening. "Hardly. It means I've been playing phone tag with Carson Donnelly and didn't check caller ID."

"Let me guess. That's somebody big in Hollywood."

"Do you hear that thudding sound? That's me banging my head against a wall. Honestly, Nik," I continue over her laughter, "considering you're friends with some of the biggest stars in LA—not to mention the city's hottest entertainment reporter—you have to start paying more attention." As billionaire Damien Stark's wife, Nikki rubs shoulders with movers and shakers in all industries, including mine. But except for projects that her friends work on, her knowledge of Hollywood caps off about the time that Hitchcock was directing Jimmy Stewart in *Vertigo*.

It's a massive character flaw in my best friend, but I've learned to live with it.

"Why should I work at paying attention when the city's hottest entertainment reporter tells me everything I need to know? Like who Carson Donnelly is."

"He, my ignorant friend, is currently the most celebrated director in town. And I interviewed him for that special I'm producing. We ended up hitting it off, and he's seriously considering casting one former actress turned entertainment reporter—initials JAH—in his next movie."

"No way!"

"Way," I say, then actually giggle. Which is pathetic because I am so not the giggling type. "I love my job, but acting is still on my bucket list. And think of the access it would give me for more interviews."

"Like you need more access. You're already the hottest entertainment reporter in town, which means every actor and director is banging down your door for an interview."

"I am awesome, aren't I?" I zip the dress and slip my feet into the waiting sandals with four-inch heels. Then I examine myself critically in the full-length mirror, and I'm pretty damn pleased with what I see.

I woke from a long nap less than an hour ago, and the puffiness that had lingered under my eyes has faded. Now I'm freshly showered, my hair falling in gleaming waves and my makeup so perfect I could audition for a Maybelline commercial. Most important for my evening plan, the dress clings provocatively in all the right places, boasts a neckline deep enough to ensure easy access to my breasts, and features a slit high enough to allow anyone sitting next to me a chance to explore parts south. Assuming, of course, that I'll let him.

I've never been one for false modesty, and as I twist and turn in front of the mirror, checking myself from all angles, I can honestly say that I look hotter than hell. Which is good, as hell-fire hot is exactly what I'm going for. I want him panting for me. I want to be that long drink of water he needs so badly it feels as if having me isn't a matter of want, but of absolute survival.

I buff my nails on my chest and realize I'm smiling. Which, considering that this extremely long day started with me stumbling under a ton of crushing worry and doubt, is a pretty terrific turn of events.

"Helloooo. Earth to Jamie."

"Oh! Hey. Sorry." I cringe, realizing I'd zoned out and completely missed everything that Nikki's been saying. "What did you say?"

"I agreed that you're awesome. And that under the circumstances, Ryan will totally forgive you for ditching his last name. Although Jamie Hunter does have a certain ring to it."

"It's tops on my list," I admit.

"But I'm worried about you, James," she continues without missing a beat. And the fact that she's using the nicknames we gave each other back when we were kids only underscores her concern. "Are you sure this is the best plan? You have to admit it's over the top, even for you. It could backfire big time."

"I better be sure. I've already set it in motion."

"So you're really going through with it." It's a statement, because Nikki knows me better than anyone. And I'm sure she can tell that my mind's made up.

"Yup." I draw a breath, feeling my bare nipples rub against the soft silk as my chest rises and falls. I think about my husband, and about how strangely distant he seemed the last time we spoke.

Ryan Hunter is more than my husband. He's my life. My soulmate. My other half. I might have been scared of the whole marriage thing once upon a time, but I was never scared of being with him. And I will happily claw the face off of anyone who tries to pry him away from me.

Bottom line, I can't imagine my life without him. More than that, I *know* him. Something's wrong. And I'm terrified that it has to do with me.

"Jamie."

"I need to stir things up." I'd made that decision after the last time I talked to him. He'd been distracted, and not just in the normal buried-in-work way. There was something else. Something that made my entire world tilt on its axis. And when he told me that he'd seen someone he once knew…well, the edge in his voice had done a number on me.

I don't understand it, but I know that it scared me. And it takes one hell of a lot to make me get scared about what's between Ryan and me.

On the other end of the line, Nikki sighs.

"If it were Damien and he was acting weird…" I trail off, leaving the idea hanging out there for her to take and run with.

"We both know what my answer is," she says. "Of course I'd do whatever it took to figure out what was going on and to fix it. I'm just not sure that what you have planned is—oh, hell, James. I only want you to be realistic. Are you sure you know what you're doing? I mean, he's out of the country for work. He's busy. It just seems—"

"I'm sure." I nod to myself, as if cementing my resolve. I have a plan, and my plan is good. Because sometimes you have to push the envelope.

There's a pause, during which I can imagine my best friend running through every possible argument in her head. But I guess none are persuasive enough because she says, "All right, then. Call me tomorrow?

Or at least text me that everything's okay."

"Will do. Swear."

"That's really the best I'm going to get out of you?"

"Pretty much."

I can picture her exasperation. Her classically pretty face scrunched in frustration as she rolls her blue-green eyes. "Fine. I'll let you go."

"Okay, bye—*oh*. I forgot to tell you. Guess who I bumped into outside the hotel?"

"That is *not* telling me," Nikki protests.

"Huh?"

"You said you forgot to tell me something. No fair making me guess. Besides, I already know. Gabby Anderson. Right?"

"How the hell did you know that?"

Gabby Anderson had come to the University of Texas for research on her graduate thesis. Something to do with medieval books. Nikki and I had been freshmen at the time, and Gabby lived in the apartment above the piece of shit place we shared. We all did laundry late at night, and that turned into drinking and talking sessions by the pool while we waited out spin cycles. I'd been bummed when she'd moved on, and though I'd genuinely meant to stay in touch, it never happened.

"She tracked me down," Nikki explains. "And said she was hoping to get together with both of us when she's back in the States. She's teaching at UT now, did you know?"

"The University of Texas *is* in the States," I point out.

"Funny. I guess she's in London on a sabbatical or something. She wasn't clear. Anyway, I told her you were on your way to London right then, and she was ridiculously excited."

"So you gave her my flight info and told her where I was staying."

"Is that bad?"

"Are you kidding? No. I always loved Gabby. But if you were trying to distract me from The Plan, it didn't work."

Nikki scoffs. "Have you made any plans with her?"

"She wanted to go have a drink tonight, but I have my own plans, obviously, and the afternoon was out because I needed a nap. Jet lag is not my friend. Honestly, I think she could have used a nap, too."

"What do you mean?"

"Teaching must be stressful because she was wound up tight. I think she probably needs someone to talk to, but I couldn't abandon The Plan."

"I think you could," Nikki chides, and I make a scoffing sound.

"The Plan is perfect," I counter. "The Plan is good. We've already had that conversation, so drop it. And Gabby hijacked my phone and put all her contact info in. I promised to text her tomorrow as soon as I'm free."

"Good. Tell her I said hi."

"Will do. And now I'm really hanging up. Got places to go and people to do."

"James…"

"Love you, Nicholas," I say, reverting to her nickname, too, and making her laugh.

"Love you back," she says, then ends the call. For a moment, I simply stand there, wondering if she's right. Maybe I am taking the completely wrong approach. But then I shake my head. I know my husband. I know what intrigues him. And what distracts him. I know how to get his motor going and erase everything else from his mind.

And I'm certain that what I have planned is going to work.

More than that, it's going to be fun.

* * * *

"Do you miss me?" I cross my legs as I lean back on the padded bench, the cool silk of the upholstery a stark contrast to the heat of my skin. A heat that has risen simply from the knowledge that he's on the other end of this line. And that he's thinking of me, too.

"Oh, Kitten, how can you even ask that?"

Ryan's voice fills my head through the small earbuds, low and rough. I feel it like a physical caress, and I press my thighs together in defense against a building storm of desire. "I want to hear you say it," I confess. "Please, Hunter. It's been too long."

"That it has." Longing fills his voice, and I close my eyes, imagining him. His chestnut brown hair. His clear blue eyes. And that lean, muscular body that fits perfectly against my curves.

"God, Jamie," he says, his voice filling out my vision of him. "I miss you desperately."

"It's horrible of me, but I'm glad to hear you say that. The last time we talked you sounded distracted, and when you said you ran into someone from your past—"

"I think my wife is jealous."

"Does your wife have reason to be?"

There's the tiniest of hesitations, and I swear my heart skips a beat. "Kitten, how can you even suggest that? I'm here for work, you know that. And it's kicking my ass. What you're hearing in my voice is exhaustion. Not infidelity."

A twinge of guilt assails me, and I start to quickly backtrack. "I didn't think—"

But then I cut myself off because maybe part of me did. Not the big part that knows and trusts Ryan. But the teeny, tiny, buried and paranoid part that may never truly believe a man like Ryan could be passionately in love with a head case like me.

"Is it terrible that I'm glad you're exhausted?"

He laughs. "Coming from anyone but you, I might be put off. But I know my wife well. And, Kitten, you know me, too. You weren't really jealous, were you?"

"How much longer will you have to stay in London?" I ask, dodging the question.

He sighs. "Hard to say. It's a monster of a project. But I think we can probably wrap up this week. Maybe ten days. We're all busting our asses over here to make that happen."

"I'm very glad to hear it."

My husband, Ryan Hunter, is the head of Stark Security, one of Stark International's newest divisions, with the mandate of providing help where needed, no matter how big or small the assignment.

That, however, is not why he's in London.

He's in the UK because before Stark Security existed, he was the Security Chief for all of Stark International, a multi-billion-dollar empire. Technically, he still holds that position. Which means that, with the exception of Damien Stark himself, Ryan is the big dog where all Stark-related security matters are concerned.

He's no longer the day-to-day guy for the whole shebang, though. Stark Security keeps him too busy for that. Nowadays, he only gets personally involved in corporate security matters when there are big things going on. Apparently the opening-month security checks and tweaks at the brand new Stark Century London Hotel is a Very Big Deal. Not to mention an overhaul of the entire security system in the London offices of Stark International.

He and Baxter Carlyle—the guy immediately under Ryan with responsibility for overseeing security in all English-speaking territories of Stark International—have been leading a London-based team for going on three weeks. Which, of course, means that they're both enjoying every luxury imaginable. Elegant suites. Incredible views. Stellar room service. An oak-paneled lobby bar with exceptional service, made better by an open expense account.

Working hard, yes. But I have a feeling the luxurious surroundings have taken some of the edge off.

As for me, I was left behind in Los Angeles. Work. Responsibilities. All that pesky adulting stuff. At first I stayed busy. But then the loneliness set in. Followed by the doubt that crept up after those few, odd phone calls with Ryan.

After that...

Well, there comes a point when a girl simply has to take action.

So I picked up my phone, and the rest is history. The fun part will be seeing where this goes. Already Hunter's voice is working its magic on me, making my skin heat and my upper thighs tingle. My nipples are already as hard as pebbles, and I know it won't take much more to really ramp me up.

And, yeah, I want to be ramped...

More than that, I have an idea of what I want next. Of which fantasies I want to live out while my husband's voice whispers in my ear. I lick my lips and rise off the padded bench and continue our conversation, lowering my voice to convey the kind of heat I'm feeling. "You miss me desperately? Define desperately. And please—be very, very specific."

His low chuckle reverberates through me, settling between my thighs. "Careful, Kitten. I'm in public. The hotel bar."

"What a coincidence," I say as I cross the tiled floor, passing men and women all dressed to the nines and ready for an evening out. "I'm in a hotel, too."

"You're not working?" I hear the frown in his voice. "I thought you were editing this week."

It's a fair question. For a while now I've been pulling exceptionally long hours doing the on-camera work and producing a series of celebrity interviews that air on various news and entertainment programs under the umbrella of Hardline Entertainment, a company owned by Hollywood mogul Matthew Holt. It's a semi-open secret that he owns a high-end sex club, and he's known around town as a total manwhore, but he's been nothing but decent to me. So decent, in fact, that he is co-producing a two-hour special on the top three box office hits last year—with me as the intrepid reporter interviewing actors and off-screen talent as we try to find the secret sauce.

It's a great project and Matthew has not only been a total gentleman, he's been downright encouraging. And he's completely respectful of Ryan. Sometimes I wonder if his manwhore, not-with-the-whole-metoo-thing rep is some sort of manufactured facade.

Then again, Ryan has the skill set to kill a man with his bare hands, and he's best friends with Damien Stark. So maybe Holt just makes a point of showing me his shiny side.

Either way, the job is great and I love it. Yes, I'd love to land the acting gig I was telling Nikki about, but after being bounced around various positions in Hollywood, I finally feel like I've landed on my feet. No matter what happens with the Carson project, I'm happy. Which makes Holt something like a ridiculously good-looking fairy godfather to me.

I turn my attention back to the call with Ryan. "I told you we finished the rough cut for the special," I say in response to his question about why I'm not in an editing booth. Granted, there is still a shit-ton of work to do. But since my words are technically one hundred percent true, I don't have to feel any guilt about lying to my husband. "And that," I add with a sultry lilt to my tone, "is why I decided to go to a hotel and call you."

"So far, I approve of your plan."

"Do you? Good. But there's a little more to it…" I let my words hang there.

"Oh?"

"See, the thing is, I'm feeling exceptionally naughty tonight."

"How interesting." There's amusement—and heat—in his voice. A heat that is definitely doing a number on my senses.

I lick my lips, then stifle the urge to cup my own breasts and stroke my sensitive nipples. I'm in public, after all. "Well, I was wondering…"

I trail off as I reach the marble pillars that mark the entrance to the dark-paneled bar. I lean against one, surveying the customers, many of whom have their backs to me. My body is thrumming with desire. I want hands. Lips. Heat. *Passion.*

Most of all, I want Ryan. But at the moment, he's not at my side.

"It's just that there are some interesting people here. Stunning women. Seriously gorgeous men." The guys in this bar are the kind of candy I would have recklessly collected back in the pre-Ryan era when I was the walking definition of a wild child. Notches on my bedpost, Nikki used to say, and always with a bit of worry in her voice. The kind of worry I ignored then. And, to be fair, I'm ignoring tonight, too.

"I'm intrigued." I hear the question in Ryan's voice even before he asks it. "What game are we playing, Kitten?"

I lick my lips, thinking of the earpiece and its tiny microphone, well-hidden under my hair. "What if I seduced one of them?"

I take a step into the room and see *him*. The one man who puts all the other customers to shame. He's sitting at the bar with his back to me, so I can't see his face. But his posture telegraphs confidence, and his short dark hair is thick. I long to run my fingers through it, imagining how silky it would feel against my skin. I can make out just a hint of his jawline—strong, with an evening shadow. I close my eyes, craving the rough feel of stubble against my inner thigh, and I actually whimper.

"Is that really what you want?" His voice is tight, but otherwise entirely unreadable.

"Is that okay?" I bite my lower lip, surprised by how fast my heart is beating. I'm genuinely nervous. More, I'm afraid he's going to deny me. "You've always said you like my wild side."

"I do," he says. "You have a man picked out?"

"Yes." I hear the breathiness in my own voice as my body sags with relief. Until right then, I hadn't realized how much I feared that he'd shut down this fantasy tonight.

"Then I think you need to do that, Kitten."

I drag my teeth over my lower lip, heat pooling between my thighs as I take a step toward the man sitting at the bar. "Are you sure?" I ask my husband.

"Have I ever denied you?"

"Never," I say, then draw an excited breath as I approach the man at the bar. He sits up straighter, as if he knows I'm behind him, and when I slide onto the empty stool next to him, he turns just enough to face me. His eyes are as blue as I saw them in my mind, and for a moment, he only looks at me, his gaze roaming over my body, the icy blue leaving a trail of heat.

I clear my throat. "This seat's not taken, is it?"

The corner of his mouth quirks up. "Would it matter if I said it was?"

"No. Buy me a drink?"

One beat. Then another. He's been focused on my lips, but now he lifts his head, then places his hand on my thigh, just above my knee. The contact sends lust curling through me, and I actually have to swallow a moan. I'm already wet and desperately turned on. And in that moment I realize exactly how much I need this night. This adventure.

His eyes lock on mine. "Why don't I have a bottle delivered to my room?"

"Oh." That was faster than I anticipated—I do enjoy the chase—but I can't say that I'm disappointed. Already, I'm imagining his hands on my skin, my dress a tattered heap on the floor.

Still, I don't want to seem too eager. I see his phone on the polished wood beside an almost empty glass, the screen face down. "Were you on a call?" I ask as I reach for his glass, then swallow the last sip of Scotch along with a few ice chips.

"I'm not anymore. You seem like a woman who'd insist on my full attention."

He slips the phone into the interior pocket of his bespoke Brioni suit, then gets off the stool and holds out a hand to help me. I slide off as well, my dress riding up, the slit revealing quite a bit of thigh. And, possibly, a quick flash of my red thong panties.

He signals to the bartender, then puts his hand on the small of my back, bare in the halter-style dress. I stifle a moan, the heat from his touch filling me. I want to say something into the microphone, to whisper in Hunter's ear about how my cunt is throbbing and my panties are already soaked. But that's not possible, and it would sure as hell destroy the moment. And so I simply stay silent as a wild and wanton heat curls through me.

The elevators are all the way across the lobby, and by the time we get there, I'm weak with desire, and if the way he's looking at me is any indication, I'm not the only one who's desperate. There's nobody else around, and when the doors open, he steps into the car, passes his room key over the control panel, then pulls me roughly toward him. I stumble into him, my breasts pressing against his hard chest as the doors close, and he pushes the button for the thirty-eighth floor.

"You must have a nice view," I say.

His mouth crooks up into a smile as his eyes look me up and down. "I do."

He takes his phone out of his jacket pocket, taps the screen a few times, then tucks the phone away again.

"What are you—"

He presses a fingertip against my lip. "Yes. My room has a nice view." He steps closer, then reaches behind me and unzips my dress, exposing my ass. I draw in a sharp gasp, my eyes automatically seeking out the small metal and glass disk mounted in the elevator's upper corner. *A security camera.*

"But—" I begin.

"No," he says. "No argument. No protest. Remember that you're the one who approached me." He puts his hands on my shoulders and slides the thin straps slowly down my arms. "This is what you want." He pauses, the bodice of the dress just barely covering my nipples. "Or am I wrong?"

I draw a breath, then exhale slowly. I glance once more at the camera, then tell myself it's okay. It has to be because I want it so much.

"Tell me," he presses.

My mouth is dry, my skin tingling, as if I've inched too close to a fire. "No," I say.

His head tilts to one side, then he raises a brow. His hands on my dress, however, don't move. "No, what?"

I lick my lips. "You're not wrong."

He says nothing, just takes a single step back, releasing the dress, which slides over my hips and falls to the elevator floor, leaving me bare except for the tiny thong. I let my purse fall, too, then draw in another breath, my heart pounding so hard he must surely hear it. But this isn't fear. This is a wild, intense, crazed need. A wanton passion that is coursing through me, making my nipples painfully tight and my sex throb in a silent, demanding plea.

"Take them off," he orders.

I do as he says, sliding the panties down, then holding the rail as I balance on one high heel so that I can step out.

He holds out his hand, and I give him the small scrap of red satin. He lifts it to his face, and with his eyes on me, breathes deep before sliding the panties into his trouser pocket. Then he leans against the elevator's far wall and slowly looks me up and down.

"As I was saying, the view from my room is nice. But this is much better." He crosses the car, needing only one long stride to reach me. One thumb brushes across my nipple, and I tremble, then gasp when he pushes me back against the wall. He shifts, one hand now cupping my neck as he holds me in place, the other sliding down between my legs.

Roughly, his mouth closes over mine, our teeth clashing and our tongues warring. He's fierce, demanding, and I close my eyes and think about the way Hunter is with me at home. Wild and bold. A man who takes what he wants even as he gives me everything I crave.

I arch back as a satisfied tremor courses through me. *Just like home,* I think. *Only decadently different.*

"You are so fucking hot," he says when he breaks the kiss. Then he steps away from me, and I moan in protest, only to swallow the sound when he flips the emergency *Stop* button on the control panel.

I expect the klaxon of the alarm, but there's no sound except his low, firm words: "I have to have you. Right now."

I can only nod, and instead of a ringing alarm the only sound that fills the car is the metallic scrape of his zipper. His cock is rock hard and perfect, just as I've seen it in my mind, and I feel my body clench in time with the chant that is filling my head—*yes, yes, yes.*

He doesn't hesitate. There's nothing uncertain or tentative about him. Instead he closes the distance between us, then runs a finger over my pussy. "You're wet," he says. "Hell, you're soaked."

"I can't imagine why," I retort. Or I try to. I half-swallow the words as he thrusts two fingers inside me.

"More," I say, but he only shakes his head and continues to finger me.

"I—"

But I don't finish the thought, because now his hands are on my waist, and he's lifting me, his strong arms pinning me against the wall. In reflex, I wrap my legs around him, and as his hands slide down to grip me at the hips, the tip of his steel-hard cock presses against my entrance. I whimper, wanting to feel him inside me, my body craving his. Needing *him.*

I arch my back, searching for a hotter, deeper contact, and at the same time, he slams his hips forward so that I'm impaled on him. He fills me completely, and I cry out from the unexpected intensity. A delicious hint of pain that is soon soothed by the familiar rhythm of a wild, fast fuck.

"That's it," he says as I ride him. "Oh, God, you feel incredible."

My speech is less coherent. My upper back is against the wall, and I'm held in place by his hand on my ass and the hard length of his cock. His other hand provides no support at all. Just the opposite, in fact, since those fingers are teasing my clit, playing me to such perfection that I'm about to spin off him and out into space.

"Come on," he urges. "Look at me, gorgeous. I want to see those beautiful eyes. I want to watch when you explode. Come on," he says, his voice as rough as our wild coupling. "Come for me now. Come *with* me now."

And, oh dear God, I do. I feel the force of his release, an explosion inside me, and it sends me over the edge. No guilt. No shame. The elevator, the hotel, the whole fucking world disappears in a storm of fire and ice that I don't ever want to end. For what feels like hours, I tremble in his arms and he holds me tight until finally, *finally,* we slide to the floor and curl up facing each other.

"Hello, Kitten," Ryan says.

"Hey, Hunter." I draw in a deep, satisfied breath as my husband strokes my hair. "I missed you too much."

"And so you came all the way to London?"

"Yup. Just picked up my phone and made an airline reservation." I slide my hand down to cup his cock. "I wanted more than just the fantasy of you."

He chuckles. "And yet you still got to play out the fantasy."

"I did. Thank you. This was deliciously wicked." I sigh, satisfied, then narrow my eyes as a question occurs to me. "How did you know it was me? When I came up behind you in the bar. You knew I was there. How?"

"Did you forget why I'm in the hotel in the first place? I had the hotel security feed streaming on my phone. I saw you walk in."

"Oh." I lick my lips, liking the idea of him watching me, then playing along the way he did. "I love you," I say.

"Do you know how magical those words are? I love you, too, Kitten." He tilts his head, his eyes narrowing as he takes my chin between his thumb and forefinger. "No one but me, Jamie. Not ever."

"Never," I agree. "You're all I want. Everything I want. Except..."

His brow creases. "Except?"

I flash an impish smile. "Except right now, I want more. Can we go to your room?"

He pulls out his phone. "Put your clothes on, baby, and I'll turn the cameras and security controls back on."

"And then?"

"And then I'm going to strip you bare all over again, tie you to the bed, and spend the rest of the night fucking my wife senseless. Assuming that's okay with her."

"Yeah," I say, smiling broadly as I hurry back into my clothes. "That's perfect."

Chapter Two

Ryan's words echo through my head all the way back to the room, making my thighs tingle and my cunt ache. The penthouse suite takes up the entire western end of the hall, and I swear it takes forever to get to the ornate double doors, then even longer for him to get inside with the key card.

By the time the door shuts behind us, my body is throbbing. Yes, he'd taken me in the elevator, but that was hard and fast and part of a game. Now I want more. I want the entire night with no make-believe.

Bottom line? I want Ryan. I want him to fuck away my fears. To completely erase the worry that had sent me running to London in the first place. And he will, too. I'm certain of it. Already I can imagine lying naked and sated in bed, Ryan's hand on my hip as we face each other, lost in delicious after-sex bliss.

Right now, though, we're still standing in the tiled entryway. It's an open floor plan, and I see a powder room off to the left, along with a hall that extends beneath a spiral staircase into mystery territory. There's a kitchenette to the right, the controls on the wine fridge glowing a soft blue that blends well with the wavy aquamarine light cast by the huge built-in aquarium.

The tank is filled with colorful, exotic fish, and even from this distance I can see the bedroom beyond. I bite back a smile, wondering if there is some sort of blind on the other side of the tank. Or if the fish—and any guests in the living room—are always allowed a watery view of whatever shenanigans might be happening in that room.

There's a huge flat screen television on the other side of the aquarium, then a stunning built-in bar that, from where I'm standing across the room, seems exceptionally well stocked.

That wall abuts the exterior wall of the penthouse, which is made entirely of glass, allowing for an exceptional view, the centerpiece of which is the London Eye. Ryan crooks his finger, and I follow as he walks that direction. Two of the glass panels pull apart, opening the living area to the balcony, and that's where we go.

The night air is pleasantly cool against my overheated skin. I stand by the modern glass barrier with the lights and majesty of London spread out thirty-eight floors below. It's so beautiful it makes my heart ache, and yet it's not what I want to see. And it's definitely not what I want to feel. I want to ache, yes, but not for the beauty or the lights or the majesty.

What I want is Ryan. I've been anticipating his touch since we stepped off the elevator, and now my skin is so primed that I'm certain I'll explode from nothing more than the feel of his fingertip against my forearm.

And yet he's not touching me at all. Damn the man.

Despite the raw, seductive words, he hasn't even kissed me, much less stripped me. And though I can imagine the feel of his hands on my bare skin, imagination is all I've enjoyed. Well, since we left the elevator, anyway.

I tilt my head and pout. "You're a tease, Hunter."

"Maybe I am." He moves toward me, then runs a strand of my hair through his fingers. He's careful not to touch my skin, and yet I shiver simply from the promise of connection. "Or maybe I'm just waiting to hear the rest of it, Kitten."

"The rest of—"

He stops me with a finger to my lips. "You're here. And it doesn't make sense."

I take a step back. "*You're* here. Of course it makes sense."

The corner of his mouth curves up, and I put a ticky-mark in the Jamie column of my mental score card.

"I appreciate the loyalty," he says. "And I definitely appreciated earlier. But that doesn't answer my question."

"Hunter, I—"

He shakes his head, silencing me. "Your work, Jamie. You expect me to believe that you dropped everything and raced to London just because you missed me? I've gone on business trips before."

"Not this long." I turn my back to him, then head toward the plush, outdoor sofa.

"True." His voice follows me, but the man himself doesn't move. "But I think we've been finding some creative ways to make up for the time and distance. Considering some of our Skype sessions, I think you could have had one hell of a career as a cam girl."

I look back at him over my shoulder. "You were already more than familiar with my wide and varied skill sets."

He chuckles. "True."

"And it's not the same."

The levity fades. "No, it's not," he admits. "And baby, I hope you know that there will never be a time when I don't prefer to have you in person. But maybe this wasn't the right time."

"Not the right time?" My mind immediately jumps to the mysterious Someone he bumped into, and I drop onto the corner of the couch, then pull a pillow to me and hug it close. "Because it's not convenient for you? What with spending every waking minute working on all those detailey security issues."

He settles into a metal and vinyl armchair that is clearly some sort of designer piece. He looks regal as fuck and totally in control. He also ignores my snide tone and not particularly subtle accusations. I'm not terribly surprised by that. I can be a real bitch sometimes. I know it. My friends know it. My husband definitely knows it. And he's learned how to ignore it.

Sometimes I'm okay with that. Right now, it's pissing me off.

He leans back. "Did you or did you not text me just the other day about how you couldn't believe that Holt was actually bringing in consultants and test audiences to screen the special before final edits?"

"So?" The word comes out cavalier. A testament to my acting skill.

My blasé attitude doesn't fool Ryan. "You gushed, Jamie. And you are not a woman from whom one expects gushing. You told me that you were giddy—and, yes, that was the word you used—about getting the chance to sit behind the one-way glass and watch the consultants interview the members of the test audience. Remember?"

"Maybe."

"Mmm. I think your exact words were *fucking amazing*. And then you made some comment about how you never realized that being a producer was like being a badass detective secretly watching an interrogation."

"Well, if I said it, I must have been drunk. The cop part. Not the fucking amazing part, because that's true."

"Giddy," he repeats. "Gushing. Hell, I smiled for days just because you were so excited. And yet here you are."

"Yeah. Here I am. With my husband. I'm sorry if that's a problem for you."

He doesn't take the bait. Instead, he stretches out his legs, totally at ease. "Were they able to move the interviews earlier?" His voice is intentionally casual, and I wish there were an equally casual response I could rattle off.

Of course there's not.

I clear my throat. "Not exactly."

"Jamie. Just tell me."

If we ever have kids, I'm pulling in Ryan and that tone whenever they get out of hand, because God knows it works. I draw a deep breath and hug my pillow closer. "I asked Matthew to have the team forward me the taped interviews. We're going to have a conference call while I'm here."

He runs his fingers through his hair, his expression perplexed. "Kitten, I don't get it. You wanted to be there. Hell, you've wanted to be in the thick of it every step of the way. You've been on cloud nine since you landed this opportunity. A two-hour special that's more than just fluff? And Matthew Holt in your corner..." He trails off, his hands rising as if he is trying to grasp the proper words.

He pushes up out of the chair, then closes the distance between us in two long strides. There's a metal and glass coffee table in front of the couch, and he sits on it, directly across from me. Then he takes my hands. But it's not a sensual touch. Instead, I see worry in his eyes. "You've been fighting to truly break in ever since you came to LA. Kitten, sweetheart, this is what you want."

I blink, and a single tear leaks out, running down the side of my nose. "But I don't want it as much as I want you." I press my lips together and look at the floor, as if that will hold back the army of tears that want to follow their leader.

"Oh, Jamie."

I hear regret and sorrow in his voice, and a cold wave of fear crashes over me. I yank my hands free, shaking my head.

"*No.*" This time, his voice is hard. Firm. He repeats it, now as soft and gentle as a kiss. "No. Oh, Kitten, Christ, I didn't realize what that mind of yours was spinning. And I am so, so sorry you were afraid. But baby, don't you know? You have me." He takes my hands again. "You will always have me."

Tears stream down my cheeks, and I suck in air, feeling both relieved and idiotic.

"Hey, hey." He moves to the couch beside me, then pulls me close. I bury my face against his shoulder, the fear I've been holding in pouring out in tears and sobs.

"You've been distracted," I say when my sobs have calmed to hiccups. "And it only got worse when you told me that you ran into someone you knew before, and my imagination started spinning, and, well, you know."

"Apparently, *you* don't know." His voice is as gentle as his touch. He stands, then lifts my chin until I'm forced to look up at him. "Things have been crazy here. I've been tasked with overseeing the installation and debugging of one security system, and the complete redesign of another, which just happens to guard a significant amount of confidential information. You know all that, right?"

I nod, feeling needy and more than a little stupid.

He takes my hands and pulls me to my feet. "But that's no excuse for being distracted and out of sorts when I talk to my wife."

"It's actually a pretty good excuse," I tell him. "And to be honest, Nikki tried to warn me."

He frowns. "Warn you?"

"That your response to my coming might not be all hugs and puppies. Because of all the work, I mean."

He shakes his head. "Never. I love that you came, and I love the way you did it. Best extra-marital seduction inside a marriage that I've ever experienced."

At that, we both laugh.

"Mostly, I love you, Jamie Archer."

"Jamie Archer Hunter," I correct.

"And thank God for that," he says.

"I love you, too," I whisper. "So, so much."

He pulls me close and kisses me, sweet and tender, as if sealing the vow between us all over again.

But when we pull apart, it's not sweetness I'm thinking about. "You know what else I'd love?"

"Knowing my wife, I could probably guess. But why don't you tell me?"

"What you promised before. Stripping me bare. Tying me to the bed. Fucking me senseless. I think that sounds just about perfect."

"Do you?"

I nod, and even though I'm not remotely shy with Ryan, I feel my cheeks warm as he slowly circles me, like a panther stalking its prey.

"Tell me why."

I swallow. That's the downside of being married to someone who truly understands me. The downside of him being Hunter. *My Hunter.* He's the man who tamed me, after all. The man who already knows the answer. He just wants me to say it out loud.

"Because I still feel raw," I admit. "Because as much as I believe that it's all about work, I can't stand feeling distant. It drives me nuts. I need to feel our connection. I need you inside me, Hunter. I want you to fuck me so hard that it feels like we're one person. I want to get so lost in each other that we have to fight our way back to reality."

For a moment, he says nothing, and I'm actually afraid I pushed too far. Then he says, "Take off your clothes."

He's behind me as he speaks, and I start to turn.

"No," he says. "Do as I say."

I bite my lip, my pulse racing. "You said you were going to strip me."

His fingers slide through my hair, and then he tightens his grip, tugging my head back with such force it's almost painful. "Arguing, Kitten?" His voice is low and sexy. Commanding. My body responds immediately, and I breathe out an excited little whimper.

"What's that? I didn't hear you."

"No." I have to force the word out past dry lips. I'm lost again, my nipples tight and my core aching. My body is a slave to this man, and I fucking love it.

"No, what?"

"No, Sir. I'm not arguing." I glance around. We're higher than any other building nearby, and the world is like a film running below us. There are no balconies on this side of the tower—only three on the building as a whole—and there's something wonderfully titillating about being naked under the night sky even while being so high I can practically touch those stars.

"Not as far to go, is there?" I ask.

"What do you mean?"

"When you make me explode. When you take me to the stars and back like you do every single time we make love." I look up at the night sky. "Not as far to travel."

He chuckles. "A fair point. Maybe tonight I should take you all the way to another galaxy."

"Yes, please."

"But only if you do as I say." He comes around to face me, then steps back and slides his hands deep into the pockets of his trousers. "Take off your clothes."

I reach back and unzip the dress, then pull the bodice down, baring my breasts just as he had in the elevator. I hold it there for a moment, then shimmy, letting the material slither over my hips to pool around my feet.

My eyes never leave Ryan's as I take a single step forward. Now I'm outside the circle of red silk, clad only in my four-inch heels. Ryan, of course, still has my panties in his pocket.

I drag my teeth over my lower lip and wait for instructions, but he says nothing. I take that as a command to continue and start to bend over to unfasten my sandals.

"No," he says, and I look up to see him stroking the bulge of his erection. "Leave them on."

I tilt my head to the side, my eyes glued to the rhythmic motion of his hand. "Do you want me to take over?"

"No," he says, and I almost laugh. Apparently, *no* is his word for the night.

He unfastens the top button of his trousers, then unzips his fly. He takes his cock out and strokes it, already thick and hard, the tip slick with pre-come. I lick my lips, wanting nothing more than to drop to my knees and take him deep in my throat.

"Spread your legs," he demands, and I eagerly comply, relishing the sensation of the air on my wet, overheated sex.

He takes a seat on the sofa, his hand still moving rhythmically up and down on flesh I want to touch. To taste.

"Finger your pussy," Hunter orders.

I can't help the moan that escapes my lips. Because even though it's Hunter's touch I crave, at the same time I can't deny that the thought of masturbating while he watches turns me on. I start with my hands on my breasts. I pinch my own nipples, then cry out as a trill of electricity shoots from my breasts to my cunt.

"Oh, Christ, baby." The rhythm of his hand on his cock intensifies. "Do you have any idea how fucking beautiful you are?"

I don't answer. Just slide my palm down my abdomen, lower and lower until my fingers cup my swollen flesh, teasing my sensitive clit. "Do you know how wet I am?"

His eyes meet mine, hot and hard. "Let me taste you."

I almost come right then, just from those words. And my nipples tighten in response as I slide my two middle fingers deep into my core. I close my eyes, my body trembling. My knees going weak. And then I ease my fingers out and take a step toward him.

I raise my hand as if offering him a taste, then draw back before he has a chance and lick my fingers. I keep my focus on Hunter and watch with satisfaction as the muscle in his cheek twitches. I look down, and I swear that his cock has gone even stiffer.

"If you want a taste," I say, "you'll have to lick something other than my fingers."

"Kitten, you know you're gunning for serious punishment, right?"

I tilt my head and smile as I slide one hand over my ass cheek, pouting a little. "Well, after all, Hunter. Don't you think I deserve it?"

Chapter Three

"Teasing me, Kitten?" There's heat and humor in his eyes, but it's his ruthless smile that sends shivers of anticipation coursing down my spine.

He's still seated, but now he rises. He zips his trousers, and my eyes are immediately drawn to the very impressive bulge. He notices, of course, and shakes his head. "You want it? Baby, you have to earn it."

"Oh." The word is little more than breath. I'm so ridiculously turned on—from his voice, from his attitude, from my own anticipation—that I can barely think. We're always good together, but it's moments like this—when he takes complete charge—that I truly understand how good he is for me. I've always been wild, and God knows I've always done what the hell I wanted, when I wanted. With Ryan, I'm doing exactly what I want—and at the same time, it is total and complete surrender. And the only reason it works is because I trust him. With my body. With my life. With my heart.

"Leave your clothes and follow me."

Without waiting to see if I've complied, he moves to the still-open glass doors, then steps over the threshold and back into the penthouse.

"Bend over, Kitten," he says with a nod to the sofa. His voice is firm, and his tone allows for no argument. It's the kind of voice that makes me melt, and I eagerly do as he says, levering my body over the back of the couch, which hits me just high enough that my bare pussy rubs the plush upholstery in a way that sends sparks all the way down to my toes.

"Hands on the cushions," he orders.

I do as he says, and he slides both hands between my thighs, urging my legs apart so that he can cup my very wet pussy before easing his hand back so that his fingers slide up the crack of my ass, sending shivers through me.

"Maybe I'll fuck you here, too," he murmurs, and my entire body clenches with longing. "Pity we don't have your collar."

"We do," I whisper. "It's in my purse."

Not long after we got together, I bolted, running more from my fear than from Ryan. He followed, thank God, and we ended up in Las Vegas. That's where things truly shifted for us, and while we were there, Ryan bought me a beautiful choker made of hammered silver—a collar. It has a loop in the front for a charm—but it's also for a leash.

Every time I wear the choker, it makes me feel special. For years, it was the physical manifestation of one very basic reality—that I belong to him. And, yes, that he belongs to me, too. It's been supplemented by our wedding rings, but not replaced. And though we've never been heavily into BDSM, we do play. But there's nothing pretend about what the collar represents.

Which is why I brought it with me to London. Because I'd wanted to hold on to that physical proof of what we are to each other as a talisman against my fears about Ryan's distraction and the mysterious person from his past.

Now, I'm even more glad I brought it. I hate that I'd doubted. That I'd been afraid. I want to make it up to him, and how better to do that than to submit utterly? To belong to him completely.

I don't turn around, but I hear him moving behind me. I'd left my purse on the table by the entrance, and I assume that's where he is. Sure enough, a few moments later he returns, his fingers lightly grazing up my spine before he pushes my hair aside and fastens the collar around my neck.

"You brought the leash, too," he says.

"Where you lead, I'll always follow. I just thought you might need a reminder."

"I don't," he murmurs, kissing my neck. "I know your heart, Jamie, just as I hope you know mine."

"I do. Truly."

"Good. Now stand up and turn around for me."

"I'm sorry I got nervous about you," I say as I follow his instructions. "About us. But I'm not sorry I came."

"Neither am I," he says, his ice-blue eyes boring into mine. "And even though I don't need a reminder, I'm still going to use the leash. Do you know why?"

"Because you like seeing me naked and bound?"

He chuckles. "I definitely do, but it's deeper than that, and you know it. It's a gift, Kitten. You're strong. Beautiful. Exceptional. And yet you surrender yourself to me. You're not just giving me power, you're giving me your trust, and every time I see you on your knees in front of me, I'm the one who's humbled."

My heart squeezes, and tears prick my eyes. Slowly, I go down onto my knees, my head down as I draw in a breath, silently offering myself to him.

He's everything, this man. Friend, lover, husband, and I'm grateful that we found each other.

Slowly, I look up at him. "The only reason I feel safe down here is because I trust you. Because you've earned it, and you continue to earn it every single day."

His throat moves as he swallows. "Jamie. I don't know if I want to hold you close to my heart or fuck you senseless."

"Both, please. But do the fucking part first."

He takes a single step back, his eyes skimming over me. I can see the change coming over him. The subtle shift from husband to master. It's sexy and delicious, and I have to fight the urge to slide my hands between my legs and feel how wonderfully wet I am.

"Stand up, then lift your chin higher."

I comply, and he bends to tie one end of the red ribbon we use as a leash to the loop on the front of the collar. It hangs all the way to the floor, the smooth satin dancing lightly between my breasts and grazing over my abdomen as I breathe slowly in and out.

Without a word, he moves behind me. He brushes my hair to the side, his fingertips grazing the sensitive skin on the back of my neck. I shiver, my entire body hyperaware of his presence. His touch. My nipples are painfully tight, my clit swollen and throbbing. I bite my lower lip, fighting the urge to beg. But I can't keep from whimpering with need.

I'm sure he hears it, but he takes no pity on me. On the contrary, he torments me even more by taking the ribbon from between my breasts. His hand brushes my skin as his fingers run slowly down the ribbon's length. He stops at my pussy, then presses his hand and the ribbon against my mons. With his hand still in place, he moves behind me.

His lips brush the curve of my ear as he whispers, "Spread your legs for me."

I do, then close my eyes in defense against the onslaught of sensation as he reaches between my legs with his free hand to grasp the ribbon, his fingers grazing lightly over my clit as he does.

He pulls the ribbon between my legs and I see stars as sparks of pleasure ricochet through my body.

Without thinking, I reach up and pinch my nipples, my breath coming hard and fast as he threads the ribbon up my back, then gives it a tug so that it teases my clit and my perineum.

I'm incredibly wet, and my hips move of their own accord, as if by wiggling I can increase the friction and make this wretched pleasure build to an explosion. Or perhaps I'll somehow work the ribbon loose and free myself from such decadent torment.

But no such luck. All I manage is to work myself into even more of a frenzy.

"Hunter," I beg. "Please."

He doesn't answer. Instead, he takes the free end of the ribbon and ties it to the collar as well, the satin strip tight enough against my sex that there is no escaping the flurry of sensations that accost me with every tiny movement and every beat of my heart.

He's never tied me like this before, and damned if I don't want more. I want it to last forever. I want to come right now. Basically, I'm nothing but want and desire and need. So is Hunter. He's moved to stand in front of me, admiring his handiwork, and the passion I see on his face both humbles and excites me.

Mostly it excites me.

So far, I've been fucked in the elevator, touched here, teased with the promise of more, and now bound so that my own breath—my own heartbeat—foments the most incredible type of torment. My sensitive skin feels as if I've been standing in a lightning storm, and all Ryan has to do is look at me and my body reacts, my pussy clenching tight against that damnable ribbon.

I'm wired and aroused, and I swear if he doesn't fuck me soon, I'll go down to the room I booked for the day, find the vibrator I packed, and take care of this intense longing myself. Except, of course, whatever I can do alone will be a poor imitation of what I want Ryan to do.

And so I simply beg.

"Please, Hunter. Touch me, spank me, fuck me. I need you. I need—

well, everything."

"You are my everything, Kitten," he says. "And you forgot that, didn't you?"

I nod, then bite my lower lip as he twirls his finger, signaling for me to turn around. "You know what I want."

I do, and I move again to the sofa, once again bending over and putting my hands on the cushions. Again, the back of the couch rubs against my pussy, but now with the ribbon moving against my body, the sensation is even more intense.

"Beautiful," he murmurs as the first light smack lands on my ass. I close my eyes, sucking in air as the sting settles through me, the pressure of the couch and the friction of the ribbon meshing with the lingering pinpricks of pain that his palm has left on my rear.

"You have the most perfectly formed ass, you know that? And I'm going to make sure you remember it's mine," he adds, rubbing away the initial burn before landing another smack. I cry out, reveling in the sting that shoots all the way down to my cunt, making me wet and wanting.

As if reading my mind, Ryan tugs on the ribbon, and I gasp, then shamelessly writhe against it. Another smack and I cry out, but my hips move as I rub my clit on this satin leash. "You're mine," he says. "Don't doubt me again."

"No," I promise. "I won't. I can't. I just missed you."

Another spank, and I cry out, then cry out again as his fingers push aside the ribbon so that he can thrust deep inside me. "Baby, you're so wet."

"I want you. I want more. Please, Hunter. I want you inside me."

What I want is for him to fill me. I want him to hold my tits as he thrusts inside me, so that I feel him front and back. So that we're close enough that I feel as though I'll melt into him.

He moves to me, his tailored slacks brushing my still throbbing ass. His hands close over my breasts, his fingers tightening on my nipples. "Is this what you want?"

"Oh, yes."

He removes one hand, then slides it down, over my belly, then lower still to my mons. He slowly curves his palm over my pussy, holding me unmoving in his hand. Then he bends closer until his entire body makes contact with my back. "No," he whispers, and I tremble beneath him.

"But—"

"No," he repeats. "Tonight isn't for you to ask. Tonight is for me to take what I want." His teeth graze my earlobe, and I wiggle my hips, shamelessly trying to get the friction just right. "You're mine, Kitten. Say it."

"I'm yours."

"To do with whatever I want. However I want."

"Yes."

"Why?"

"Because I trust you."

"Do you? Jamie, do you trust me?"

I frown, something in his tone cutting through the sensual haze filling my mind. But before I can say anything, he continues.

"Do you trust me to take care of you? To make you explode? To fulfill your deepest fantasies?"

"Yes."

"Do you trust that I would never hurt you?"

"God, yes."

"And do you know—really *know*—how much I love you?"

"I do. Truly."

"Are you sure, Kitten?"

I hesitate, because hadn't I come here because of exactly those kinds of doubts? But I never doubted that he loved me. Just that—I don't even know what I thought, and now that I'm here in his arms, it doesn't even matter.

"Jamie?"

"I'm sure," I say. "I've never been as sure of anything as I am of you."

His hand on my pussy tightens almost imperceptibly, but it's still enough to send a shiver running through me. "Then go to the bedroom," he says, stepping back and breaking the connection between our bodies. "Eyes closed, Kitten. On your back. Arms stretched wide, legs spread. And baby, no peeking."

"Or you'll punish me?" I twist around so that I can see him behind me, my voice flirty.

He rakes his eyes over me, his gaze stern. "Oh, yeah. I'll punish you by stopping."

I make a face, my eyes dipping to that telltale bulge in his pants. Punishing me would be punishing him, too. But I know he'd do it. In part to win, but mostly to keep me on edge and make the explosion next time that much sweeter.

I, however, am greedy, and I don't want to wait until next time. Which is why I do as he says and go to the bedroom. I sit first, then scoot back until my feet are on the mattress. Then I lie back and stretch my arms out, my fingertips almost reaching the sides of the king-size bed. I spread my legs so wide that my inner thighs burn. I'm still wearing the collar and the ribbon, and I close my eyes, biting my lower lip as I imagine Hunter's view. Except for that thin strip of red, I'm fully exposed, completely vulnerable to my husband. My Hunter. And, yes, I love it.

"No peeking," he orders, as the mattress shifts with his weight. I nod, just a slight motion of my chin, then suck in air as I feel the quick lick of his tongue over my nipple followed by a cool stream of air that has me arching up, silently begging for more.

He doesn't disappoint—his fingertips trail gently over my belly, followed by the tip of his tongue and his lips as he kisses, licks, and tastes his way down, down, down, until I'm panting with anticipation and trying desperately to widen my legs, craving his hot mouth and busy tongue on my cunt.

He kisses me lower and lower, then flicks the tip of his tongue over my clit. That, however, is only a tease. Because he moves quickly over my needy core to tease my inner thighs with the stubble on his usually clean-shaven jawline. It feels like heaven, and I rock my hips, wanting more, craving his breath on my center, his tongue, his heat.

And then—*oh, yes*—his finger tugs the ribbon aside as his mouth closes over my clit. He starts slow, but soon he's sucking the hard, swollen nub, making my core contract in a silent demand as I beg him to use his fingers, his cock. I just want to feel him inside of me.

"Patience, Kitten," he murmurs, releasing his intimate hold just enough that I'm teased by his breath as he speaks. "I've found a pretty pearl." Another lick. "I'm a very lucky man."

"A mean man," I counter. "Why don't you make me a lucky girl and fuck me?"

He laughs, then uses his palms to push my knees up, exposing me even more. His fingertip teases my ass as his tongue laves my perineum all the way up to my clit, sending electrical threads of longing coursing through me. I'm shaking, my body rocking and demanding with such intensity that he has to work hard to hold my legs in place. But I can't help it. I'm over the edge. I'm past sanity. I need to be fucked. I need to let go.

"Patience, Kitten. Do you really think I'd leave you unsatisfied?"

"Please. God, Hunter, I can't stand it."

"You can."

I shake my head. Then nod. Then shake it again, all the while murmuring *please, please, please.* I no longer know what city I'm in or if I'm even still tethered to Earth. But I do know that he's right. I can stand it. Hunter knows my limits—he always has. With him, it's always one hundred and ten percent—or more. And though I'm not entirely sure I can survive that *more,* I do trust my husband. And right now, I'm swimming on wave after wave of bliss, and I haven't even come yet.

"Good girl," he murmurs, and as his thumb strokes slow circles on my clit, his mouth eases down my leg and then, God help me, he slips off my sandal and draws my big toe into his mouth. This is new, but oh, holy fuck, the sensation is incredible, and I lose myself in bliss as he sucks me down even further under a tidal wave of need and craving and desperation.

"Like that?"

"Yes. Oh, God, yes."

"Good. Because—"

The sharp *ba-ching* of a text to his corporate phone interrupts, and he curses, then mutters an apology about a server test. I hear him slide to the edge of the bed, then snatch up the phone. Almost immediately, he curses again, hard and sharp, and I mentally do the same, because if there's a crisis at work, he'll have to go in. And that is not the way I want this evening to end.

I know I shouldn't, but I open my eyes, then shut them immediately before he catches me breaking that rule. But they were open long enough for me to see his face. Frustration, yes. But not just because of the interruption. Instead, I think I see fear.

But that makes no sense. Ryan's the type to be energized by work, no matter how big the challenge. I can't ask, though, because I'm not supposed to be looking, and I try to appear innocent, desperately pretending that I saw nothing at all.

Ping!

This time it's his personal phone, and as Hunter curses, I peek at him again. He crosses the room to the table where he'd left it, reads the text, then sucks in air before he tosses the phone back onto the table. For a moment, he stands perfectly still. And when he does start to turn, I close my eyes.

A moment later, I open them, pretending it's the first time. His expression is unreadable. A mask.

"Hunter? What is it?" I prop myself up on my elbows and watch as he hurries into his clothes. A cold chill washes over me, and I grab the edge of the comforter and pull it over my bare legs. "Ryan?"

"It's nothing. Just some work stuff I thought could wait. It can't."

I swallow, then pull the blanket higher to cover my breasts. "Will you—"

"I'll be back as soon as I can."

He barely looks at me. But as soon as he's dressed, he grabs his work phone, then hurries to the door. He pauses, then glances back at me. "I love you, Kitten," he says, coming over to kiss me on the cheek. "I love you so damn much."

I'm reeling at his change in attitude. But before I can ask, he takes a breath and hurries out, leaving me wondering what the hell is going on.

I'm still wondering after I've slid off the bed and wrapped myself in the hotel robe. I sit back on the edge of the mattress, thinking that maybe I'll order one of the hotel's adult movies, just to take the edge off, when I realize that Hunter walked off without his personal phone. I pick it up, and the face recognition feature causes the screen to pop on immediately. Not odd, since we added each other to our phones months ago, but I gasp anyway.

Not in surprise that I have access. No, I'm gasping in shock at the text that's now staring me in the face. A text from a number I don't recognize.

I'm sorry I ran from you.
But please believe me—
I need you again, Ryan. Now. Desperately.
Our last kiss burns in my thoughts.
You know what it meant for both of us.
Meet me at the same place.
Don't let me down.
Love, F

Chapter Four

Goddamn fucking son-of-a-bitch!

Ryan pressed the call button for the elevator a second time, as if that would do anything, then forced himself to step back and lean against the wall.

After all, someone on his team might be monitoring the elevator bank, and even if the feed was unwatched, he hardly wanted a permanent memento in the video vault of him losing his shit. He needed to try to look like everything was normal.

But it wasn't. Everything had stopped being normal three days ago.

That, he thought as he stepped onto the elevator, was when things had gone completely off the rails.

And, yes, that was when he should have called and told Jamie everything. But how could he when he hadn't understood what the fuck *everything* was? When he still didn't understand?

All he knew for sure was that three days ago, he'd gotten a text on his work phone from someone who insisted that Ryan come to a meeting at a pub near Marble Arch.

You helped me a long time ago. Now I need you again. Will explain in person. Please don't let me down.

Curious and concerned that the mysterious text might be connected to one of Stark Security's pending cases, Ryan had gone to the pub. But no one had been waiting for him.

He'd stayed for fifteen minutes, hoping the contact would show, before he spoke with the hostess.

"You must mean the lady who left the note," the hostess had said. "She told me a guy with dark hair and blue eyes might ask about it." As she spoke, she reached into a drawer and passed Ryan one of the pub's napkins.

He'd glanced down, then frowned at the two neatly formed words: *I'm sorry.*

"Did she say anything else? Did you see which direction she went? Did she pay with a credit card?"

"No, she didn't say a thing other than describing you. And she actually went out the exit in the back through the kitchen," she added, pointing behind her. "Said she was going to the restroom, then suddenly the damn alarm's going off."

"How about a credit card?"

"I don't know, but I couldn't tell you her name even if she did. I mean, that's—"

"A moot point unless she used a card," Ryan had said. "Can we at least find out? If she did, I'll speak to your manager. If she didn't, maybe I can at least chat with her waiter."

Her nose had wrinkled, but she'd nodded, then gestured for a tall man with bright flaming red hair to come over.

"Can I help you?" he'd asked in a voice thick with an Irish lilt.

The hostess had explained, and the waiter shook his head. "Cash. Good tip, though."

"Did you speak to her at all?" Ryan had asked.

"Just to take her order. Red wine and chips. And water. Why? What's going on?"

"Don't worry about it, Tommy," the hostess had said, then added to Ryan, "I'm sorry. This is about more than getting stood up, isn't it?"

He'd handed her a business card. "If you see her again, I'd appreciate a call."

Her lips pursed, but she'd nodded. "Doubt I will. She wasn't a regular. But good luck."

He'd thanked her, headed out the door, and circled around to the back alley. But there'd been no sign of the woman. All he'd had left was the sick feeling in his gut that someone in trouble had turned to him for help, and that he'd had no way to find her and no explanation why she'd abandoned the meeting that she'd asked for.

But if she'd expected him to walk away and forget it, she was sorely mistaken. Because the whole incident had gotten under his skin. Was she a witness? A victim? Someone looking for help from Stark Security?

Whoever this mysterious friend was, he'd been determined to track her down and figure out what was going on. Texting her back hadn't gotten him an answer, not that he'd expected it would. And when he'd run a trace on the number, he'd learned that it was a burner, not attached to anybody.

Without anything else to go on, he'd called in Baxter Carlyle, his second in command. Baxter had immediately gotten to work, and soon Ryan had video of her leaving from a neighboring store's security camera. The quality was for shit, but Ryan had recognized her build, the angles of her face, even the way she walked.

He knew her; dear God, he knew her.

Felicia.

There hadn't been a doubt in his mind. The woman on the video—alive and well—was the same woman he'd watched get shot in the gut and tossed off a train into a raging river.

The woman he'd failed more than a decade ago.

The wife who couldn't possibly be there.

And yet that had been her image on the tape. Her, or maybe someone impersonating her?

But how?

More important, why?

Now, in the hotel elevator, the tightness in his gut that he'd been battling ever since he'd seen that video returned in full force. A tightness that had only completely faded when Jamie had come to him in London, playing the game that was so very Jamie. A game that made him smile as much as it made him hard.

A game that had let him escape from his fears and worries for just a little bit.

Christ, what the hell was he going to tell Jamie?

As the elevator doors slid open and he stepped into the lobby, he could imagine her voice. *Everything, Hunter. Tell me every fucking detail right this second. Turn around, come back to the room, and tell me what the fuck is going on.*

Except he didn't know what the fuck was going on. Didn't know the repercussions of Felicia coming back from the dead. Didn't know what she even wanted.

He thought about her text: *I need you again, Ryan. Now. Desperately.*

Was it his help she needed? Or was it *him*?

A fist seemed to tighten around his heart, his mind whirling with possibility. He needed to think clearly, dammit. Needed to be logical. To rely on his training.

His long strides ate up the ground as he crossed the lobby, his attention only on the door, with not even the slightest glance toward any of the hotel staff. Walking helped, his thoughts clicking into place. The first thing he needed to question was whether the woman even was Felicia. She looked like her, of course, and the carefully worded text suggested that she was.

He thrust out his hand to hail a cab, his thoughts churning as he slid inside and gave the address of the pub.

If it was Felicia, that meant she'd survived. Which raised dozens of questions, right there. Her injury had been bad enough, but the fall alone would have been enough to kill her. If she was alive—and it damn sure looked like she was—then maybe everything that happened on the train was an elaborate extraction.

And if that was the case, then Felicia had never been an innocent girl who hooked up with the wrong guy. She'd been in intelligence, and Ryan had gotten thrust in the middle of God only knows what. Had she been complicit in Mikal Safar's murder? In the coup itself?

Hard to believe, but he'd worked in intelligence long enough to know it was possible. And pretty much the only option for her to have not only survived but to have remained hidden for so long.

And what about the alternative? What if the woman was an imposter? Well, that raised different questions. Why would someone do that? More importantly, why contact Ryan?

Blackmail? About what?

Revenge? For what?

Was there someone out there who blamed him for Felicia's death? Maybe, though he couldn't imagine someone who blamed him more than he already blamed himself. After all, her own father was already dead. But immediately after the failed mission—even while he was still in the hospital—Ryan had told Randall everything that had happened in excruciating detail. He felt he owed it to the man.

Randall had never once suggested that Ryan was to blame. On the contrary, he'd thanked him for trying to help, and apologizing that he'd unwittingly sent Ryan into a hornet's nest on the verge of exploding.

Of course, Randall Cartwright did have a stepbrother with whom he'd been close. Perhaps William blamed Ryan for the loss of his niece? Maybe. But why wait all these years to do anything about it? He shook his head; he didn't know.

And the bottom line was that he wouldn't have a single answer until he met with the woman, which was exactly why he'd run out on his wife and was heading to the pub right now, this very moment, before she could bolt again.

And, yes, he knew that the odds were good that he was about to get wrapped up in one hell of a shit storm. And yet...

He couldn't ignore that tiny whisper of hope. Because if Felicia had survived—if she'd come to him for help—then he'd just been handed a second chance.

Maybe it was a setup. But maybe she was truly in trouble. And he couldn't turn his back on that. Not when it might be serious. Not when this might be his chance to make right what had gone horribly wrong all those years ago.

An opportunity to repair the biggest clusterfuck of his professional career. To ease his guilt.

But at what price?

Because the bottom line was that he didn't know a goddamn thing.

That reality smacked hard against him, and his blood ran cold. *Not a goddamn thing.* Not even if Jamie was legally his wife. Because if Felicia was alive, what did that mean?

Oh, Christ, no. Please, no.

He drew in a breath, pausing for a moment as a wave of renewed guilt swept over him. He hadn't said a word to her about Felicia. Not about the first aborted contact. Not about what he'd seen on the video footage. Not about the text he was now chasing. Not even about that mission so many years ago.

And to top it off, he'd flat-out lied about his reason for walking out on her now, manufacturing a fake work crisis.

He'd never done that before. *Never.* And he knew damn well that he needed to tell her the truth. All of it.

But somehow he couldn't manage to make that call.

Because right then, there were only two things he knew for certain. First, that their world was poised on a knife edge. One tip in the wrong direction, and they'd go spinning off into the abyss.

And second, that Jamie could easily push them past that breaking point. Because if he knew his wife at all—and he damn sure did—he knew that she was going to go completely off the rails. And while Ryan might be a man who liked to be in control of his surroundings, he'd learned a long time ago that he couldn't control Jamie Archer. Not fully. Not really.

Despite everything, his lips curved into a smile. Because that was what he loved the most about her. That wicked independence. A delicious wildness that only he could tame. Because he was the only one she'd ever allowed to tame it.

So, no.

He couldn't tell her. Not yet, anyway. And not only because the situation would undoubtedly spawn an explosion, but also because he knew enough to know that if the woman *was* Felicia—and if she'd crawled out of the grave to find him—that meant that there was something out there a hell of a lot scarier than hiding under the cloak of a faked death.

Maybe he was justifying his silence, but there was a logic to his bullshit.

The taxi pulled to a stop and he passed the driver the fare, then stepped out onto the sidewalk, for the second time standing in front of that same pub near Marble Arch. This time, he'd get answers.

And, yes, coming here was the right decision, no matter how much keeping such a fraught secret from Jamie ate at his gut. At least it was only for an hour or so. As soon as he got back to the hotel, he'd sit her down and explain the whole thing.

What he knew.

What he didn't know.

All the answers he'd intended to get when he reached the pub. Like who the woman really was—Felicia or someone impersonating her.

Why she'd bolted that first time, and why she'd contacted him again tonight. Twice, for that matter. First on his work phone with a text that simply said, *I'm sorry I bailed before. But need to talk. Same place. Please. Urgent.*

Straightforward, and he would have gone based on that text alone, if for no other reason than he wanted answers. Including how she'd gotten his direct work number.

But then the second text had come in. The text signed by F. That mentioned a kiss. That said she needed him.

If he hadn't already been halfway out the door, that one would have pushed him over the threshold.

That one had come to his personal phone, as if she had to make sure he didn't miss either text. As if—

He froze.

Oh, fuck. His personal phone.

He'd left his phone in the suite.

In the suite. With Jamie.

For a moment he just stood there outside the pub, all of his options running through his head. He had to explain now. Or at least try to.

But dear Christ, what the hell was he going to say?

He didn't know, but he had to say something.

Before he could change his mind, he pulled out his phone and dialed her number.

Three rings...and then it kicked to voicemail.

He hung up, then tried again, knowing damn well that the call was going through. Even if she'd silenced her phone, it was programmed to always ring if Ryan was calling from the business account. Considering his line of work, he'd insisted on having a way to reach her in an emergency no matter what.

Which meant her obnoxious ring tone was blaring through the suite, and she was ignoring it.

And *that* meant that she must have picked up his personal phone and seen the message.

Fuck.

This time, when he called again, he waited through her voicemail message. "Kitten, it's not what you think. I need you to trust me for another hour or so, and I swear I'll tell you everything. I love you, baby. Just please, wait for me to get back."

Hardly adequate, but right then it was the best he could do. He was already at the pub, and the sooner he met with Felicia, the sooner he'd have answers and be on his way back to Jamie.

He stepped through the door, looked around, and felt the cold bite of frustration when he didn't see Felicia anywhere.

Chapter Five

Ryan's been gone less than five minutes, and already I've read the whorish bitch's text over a dozen times.

I need you again.
Our last kiss
What it meant
The same place
Love, F

The words burn inside my mind, and I want to vomit.

She needs him desperately?

Their last kiss?

And what fucking place?

I'm not sure if none of it makes sense, or if I'm just too numb to process the words. Or to process my thoughts, for that matter.

How can I, when all I feel is dead?

I've been pacing the suite, and now I realize that I've stopped in front of the open balcony door. I have the phone in my hand, and I'm about to hurl it off into space when I force myself to stop.

For one, I don't want to give some unsuspecting pedestrian a concussion. For another, I don't actually want to let it go. It's the smoking gun. The proof of his lies. His infidelity. And, goddammit, I want to shove it hard up his lying, cheating ass the moment he walks through that door.

Except...

Except maybe I don't. This is Ryan, after all. My Hunter. Could he have done this to me? To us?

Fuck.

The curse is lame. A whisper in my head. And I wipe away the tears that now cling to my lashes.

With a watery sigh, I move back to the sofa and drop down onto one of the overstuffed cushions. Then I open his phone and read the text one more time.

I'm sorry I ran… need you again… desperately… our last kiss…

Fuck, fuck, fuck.

And you know what else? Fuck all of this. I'm not going to just sit here with a smoking gun and do nothing.

So I tap the number at the top of the screen, put the phone on speaker, and wait for the bitch who's probably fucking my husband to answer the line.

One ring. Two. Five. Eight.

It never goes to voicemail. Just rings and rings and rings.

I end the call, then stare at the phone as I transfer the whole of the sense of betrayal I'd been feeling about Ryan to this palm-sized collection of plastic and silicon. Without thinking, I hurl it across the room, and it smashes against the wall. I know the things are damn near indestructible, but that at least felt good.

With a little bit of the weight relieved, I snatch my own phone from off the coffee table. I hit the speed dial for Nikki, not even thinking about the time difference. It's only when the call rolls to voicemail that I wonder if it's the middle of the night there. But, no, London is ahead of California. It's almost ten here, which means it's…lunchtime there?

Maybe. I'm not sure. I can't do math right now. But if it's during work hours, she's probably busy.

I start to leave a whiny message but think better of it. Instead of the rant I want to leave, all I say is, "Sorry. Didn't mean to call. Hope all is awesome in La-La Land."

It's lame, but knowing Nikki, if I'd filled her in, she'd get on one of the Stark jets and actually fly over here to both commiserate with me and to make sure I don't do anything rash—like whack Ryan's nuts off—without being absolutely certain he's cheated.

And if he has, then in true best-friend fashion, she'd help me castrate the motherfucker.

But Hunter? Do we actually believe that?

That little voice is back in my head, but I'm so angry I don't want to hear it.

I need to talk. Need to get out of my own head. Usually when I'm like this, Nikki is my go-to gal. And Ryan is my go-to guy.

Which leaves me hanging out on a limb with my ass flapping in the wind.

Shit.

I stalk to the far side of the room and retrieve Ryan's phone. The screen is cracked, but otherwise it seems to be okay. I shove it in the pocket of the spa-style hotel robe I'm wearing. Not as satisfying as burning it, maybe, but probably more practical.

I consider calling Ollie to commiserate with. He's the third part of my friend trifecta—him, Nikki, me—but he's got a relatively new job with the FBI and is at some seminar in DC. Plus, this is a crisis that needs a girlfriend. And while I love Ollie to death, dealing with relationships has never been his strong suit.

I could try to get my mind off of this with work. I could try to reach Carson Donnelly. Or I could log on to the server and review some of the edits the team is working on.

But I'd just fuck it up. Because my mind is *so* not on work.

Once again, I open the text. Because, obviously, I am a complete and total masochist. Except I'm not. On the contrary, I'm a foolish, cockeyed optimist because I'm still harboring the fantasy that this time the note will make sense. This time, I'll have an *aha* moment and everything in my universe will right itself.

Like, *aha!* I'd totally forgotten that he was doing that routine at a comedy club involving a skit about cheating on his wife.

Or, *aha!* Space aliens got tired of sucking humans up into their ships for experiments, so they stole Ryan's phone in order to mindfuck me and analyze my responses.

Or *aha!* This is a badly conceived plan for some wild and crazy sexy times.

Or some other ridiculous idea. I know the idea must be ridiculous because there's no reasonable explanation for the text.

None that I want to believe, anyway.

My gut twists as I remember all those sweet words he said to me. Trust. Surrender. Humbled.

And he called me smart?

What kind of bullshit is that? Because clearly I'm stupid and blind and ridiculously naive.

But am I? Am I really? I've always trusted Ryan without hesitation, knowing with absolute certainty that he's a good man. Which means this isn't possible. Ryan can't be—

God, I can't even think the word.

And who the *fuck* is F?

I expel a loud, frustrated breath, then shake myself. I'm going around and around in circles, and I need to get off this carousel of doom. Hell, I need to get out of this hotel.

And that's when it hits me—the perfect distraction.

I snatch up my own phone and search my contacts for the number Gabby put in. I press the button to connect the call, then hold my breath, hoping she's available.

"Jamie?"

"Hey!" My voice comes out with far too much energy. "Sorry, I'm just happy I caught you."

"Me, too. What's up?"

"Turns out my husband's working and I'm sitting here bored in the hotel." A lie, yes, but at least it's a little one. "Any chance you want to grab that drink now and play catch up?"

"Oh. Well…"

I deflate. "You have plans."

"No. I mean, yes. I mean, I got stood up. I'm actually in a cab right now. I was going to just head back to my hotel and drown my sorrows in whatever cheap wine is in the minibar. But your plan is better. Do you want to meet somewhere?"

"That would be fabulous."

We settle on a nearby wine bar, and I'm just about to hang up when the call-waiting beeps.

It's Ryan.

My first instinct is to take it. But I don't. I don't want to hear excuses and explanations. I don't want to filter truth from lies.

I don't want to have to fucking deal with any of it.

Honestly, right now, all I want is to get a drink.

And I'm going to do exactly that. With Gabby.

Chapter Six

I'm only a five-minute walk from the cute little bar that faces Hyde Park. But with getting dressed and out of the hotel, and then navigating the unfamiliar streets of London, she still beats me there. The place is Paris-themed, with an outdoor seating area, and I see her right away at a small table under a red awning. She has pale skin contrasted by hair so dark it's almost black. It's thick, with just a hint of curl, and her wide, slanting eyes are highlighted by perfectly arched brows.

She's scanning the passersby, her expression intent. Since I assume she's looking for me, I wave and hurry over, then slide into the spindly little chair with the woven wicker seat across from her. "This place is adorable," I say.

A waiter approaches with a carafe of red wine, and I cock an eyebrow. "Great service, too."

She laughs. "I went ahead and ordered wine. I hope you still like red. I remember you did in college."

"Red's great, and I'm impressed. I have no memory at all of what you drank."

"What can I say? I'm a detail kind of girl. Any food?" she asks, looking first at my face and then off to the side, as if she can't stop taking in the view.

I realize that I haven't eaten in ages. "Actually, that would be great." The waiter recommends the charcuterie and cheese plate, and we enthusiastically agree. Then, as he heads off to put in our order, Gabby leans over and draws me into a hug.

"I'm glad you called," she says. "You have no idea. I couldn't believe it when Nikki said you were in London, too. I've been—" She breaks off with a quick shake of her head, her finger tracing the rim of her wine glass. "Sorry. Not the time, not the place."

"What's going on?"

"Just, you know. Life crap. I want to hear about why you're in London. Vacation? Work?"

"Honestly, I came to surprise my husband. *But,*" I say before she can ask me about Ryan, "what is it you're not telling me?"

"What? Nothing." Her face flushes as she takes the carafe and tops off her wine glass.

"Hey, whatever it is, it's not my business. And I get that we haven't even spoken in forever. But that doesn't mean I never thought about you. Or stopped caring. If you don't want to talk about it, that's fine. But just know that you have a friend if you need one."

She meets my eyes for just a second before looking down again. "That means a lot. It's—it's just—"

This time, when she looks up, I see tears in her eyes.

"Gabby." I take her free hand. "It's okay. Whatever it is, it'll be okay."

She shakes her head, and this time when she looks at me, I see fear. "I don't think so." Her voice is low, almost a whisper. "I'm scared, Jamie."

"Can you tell me why?" I'm not usually a soft and gentle person, but my voice right now would soothe a rampaging bear. I'm terrified she's going to bolt before I can find out enough to actually help her, and right now I don't have any idea what the problem could be. Is she broke? Pregnant? Is her boyfriend abusive?

The only thing I *do* know is that I must be a truly horrible person. Because right now, I'm glad for the reminder that whatever is going on with Ryan, I'm not the only one with problems.

I squeeze her hand gently. "Come on, Gabs. I can't help you if you don't tell me."

"I don't think you can help me at all." A tear clings to the end of her nose before falling with a *plop* onto the tiled tabletop. Her shoulders rise and fall as she takes a breath. Slowly, she lifts her head. "I thought maybe I could tell you because—well, it doesn't matter, does it? Because even if you could help, I'm not sure if I should say anything."

"Of course you should. And of course I'll do whatever I can to help."

She shakes her head. "They might find out."

"They? Who?" I've gone suddenly cold, my body tense from the larger message in her words. "Someone is after you. Who?"

"That's just it. I don't know." She wipes more tears away, then downs her entire glass. I take a large gulp from mine. Frankly, I need it.

"Listen, Gabby. You're obviously scared. But my husband works in security. If someone is trying to hurt you, let me help. Tell me what's going on."

She bites her lower lip.

"Come on, girl. It's me. You can trust me. You know that, right?"

She nods, looking miserable. "I have a confession," she says, so softly I almost can't hear her. "I already knew your husband did that kind of work."

"Oh." I'm not entirely sure what to do with that information.

"The thing is..." She trails off, then takes a sip of water before starting over. "The thing is, I didn't call Nikki out of the blue."

I lean back, my eyes wide. "You totally researched me and Ryan."

"Not researched so much as followed. I saw your picture with Nikki a while back and just started paying attention." Her voice is as sheepish as her expression. "It wasn't like I was stalking. After all, you move in some pretty public circles."

"Friends with Damien Stark," I say, because this one I'm used to. "I get it."

"Well, yeah, but I meant on your own. All the stuff you do in Hollywood. The celebrities you've interviewed. And some of the articles talk about your husband, too. And then all this stuff happened, and I remembered him. And so I called and—"

"It's okay. I get it. This wasn't about chilling with me. It was about Ryan all along. But why did you need him? Is there someone you're afraid of?"

Her eyes dart around, taking in our surroundings before focusing on me. "It's—" She doesn't finish. Instead, she shoves her chair back and stands. "I—I'm sorry. I shouldn't have dragged you into this. I should—I should go."

"Gabby, no!" But it's no use. She just shakes her head and hurries out onto the sidewalk. I realize I'm standing, and I call her name, but she's gone, and I have no idea why. Then I think about her being afraid, and the way she kept scanning the sidewalks. I whip around to look behind me, suddenly worried there's someone standing with a gun at the spot she just vacated.

But there's no one there. No one except Ryan, who grips my upper arms with both his hands. "Who was that?" he asks, his voice low and dangerous. "Tell me right now who the fuck you were talking to."

Chapter Seven

I have one hell of a temper. Always have, probably always will.

I've been known to scream, throw things, slam doors, and occasionally get off a good, old-fashioned punch. I've chilled a bit over the years, but I've always been a bit of a wildcat. Nikki used to tell me that it was good I wanted to be an actress, because then I'd have someplace to channel the big personality.

Right now, though, I don't scream. I don't yell. I don't toss my wine in his face. Instead, I just look at him. I just stare him the fuck down.

"*That's* what you have to say to me?" I practically spit the words. "Some bitch sends you a text about hooking up, and *I'm* the one who needs to explain about going out and meeting a friend? Fuck you."

"Dammit, Jamie, who was she?" His tone is harsh and urgent, but I recognize the guilt in those eyes I know so well, and all of my earlier lectures to myself about trust and explanations vanish in a puff of fury laced with bone-deep sadness.

"Who. Was. She." He repeats each word slowly, but I say nothing. Not even when he sits in Gabby's abandoned seat. Not even when he says, his voice gentle, "Please, Jamie. It's important."

I can only shake my head. My throat feels clogged, but I blink ferociously, willing myself not to cry. I'd been feeling better for a few moments, with my mind on someone else's problem. But now it's as if I've been kicked in the gut all over again. As if the world and everything solid and real in it has just been ripped away. The magician's tablecloth trick gone horribly wrong, sending all the beautiful, perfect crystal and china crashing to the floor.

Humpty Dumpty, right? Because who could possibly put that back together again?

A giggle escapes from my throat, and in some coherent part of me I think, *Oh. So this is what it means to be hysterical.*

But it doesn't matter. It's only a notation. A footnote on the moment.

In front of me, Ryan rubs his temple, then draws a breath. "Jamie, please. I asked you to trust me. I told you I'll explain everything. Didn't you listen to my voicemail?"

I manage to shake my head.

He sighs, then reaches for my hand, but I flinch away. His eyes widen, the response so subtle that I'm probably the only person on earth who would even notice it. But I do. Because I know him well. So very fucking well.

At least that's the joke. I'm still not entirely sure what the punchline is.

"I told you to trust me. I told you I'd explain everything. Kitten, we need—"

"Do *not* call me that." The words snap out of me with the force of a whip.

And then I sag, suddenly empty.

But it isn't my anger that's drained me—it's Ryan. What he did. What he kept from me.

I shake my head, feeling numb. "I can't," I say.

"Dammit, Jamie, you can. Who were you with right now? Are you safe? Tell me what happened."

Safe? I've never felt this wounded in my life. Confusion and helplessness whirl inside me. I don't even want explanations anymore. Not now. I don't want to talk. I don't want anything except sleep. "I can't," I repeat. "I can't do this right now."

With a defeated shake of my head, I toss a fifty pound note on the table then turn toward the sidewalk. I keep my eyes down until I'm away from the restaurant, then I lift my chin and walk toward the hotel, as if I'm just one more woman out on a stroll tonight. I may be broken, but I'm damn well not going to show it.

Ryan says nothing, but I know he's behind me.

I go all the way back to the hotel, the words in my head keeping in time with my steps. *Trust him. Trust him. Need. To. Trust. Him.*

Over and over until we're both back in the elevator. The same elevator we were in just a few hours ago.

And that's it. That's the last burden that I can bear.

My knees go weak. My back slides down the wall. And I end up on my ass, my arms encircling my legs as I put my forehead on my knees and bawl like the big baby I am.

He kneels in front of me. "Jamie, please. I did call. And I told you I'd explain when I got back. It's not what you think."

My head snaps up. "Explain?" I tug his phone out of my purse, and the screen flashes on, revealing that toxic message. I thrust it toward him. "How the hell do you explain something like this?" I'm seething again. But at least anger is better than collapsing into a pile of pitiful goo.

He doesn't take the phone right away, and when he finally reaches for it, he moves carefully, like a hunter stalking a ferocious animal. But I don't know what he's afraid of. Maybe he's always called me Kitten, but even as angry as I am, at the moment I feel as if I've been thoroughly and painfully declawed.

He takes it gingerly from my fingers, then glances at the screen. I know exactly what he's seeing:

I'm sorry I ran from you.
But please believe me—
I need you again, Ryan. Now. Desperately.
Our last kiss burns in my thoughts.
You know what it meant for both of us.
Meet me at the same place.
Don't let me down.
Love, F

Those words will be forever etched in my brain. I think of them now, and a chill runs up my spine. *Someone walking on my grave.* That's what my grandma would say. I think it fits. God knows I feel like I'm dying. And every second that Ryan stays silent, I die a little bit more inside.

"You weren't supposed to see this."

"Oh, gee. You think?" I hear the pain and sarcasm in my voice, and it gives me hope. Maybe I'm not as numb as I thought. Maybe I'm going to be able to put up a fight.

Too bad I don't know what—or who—I'm fighting.

The elevator slides to a stop and as the doors open, I get back on my feet, ignoring the hand Ryan holds out in a silent offer of assistance.

I step out ahead of him and march to the room. I open the door, walk inside, and then let the heavy door fall back into place. He catches it before I hear the satisfying clunk of the door slamming in his face.

"*Jamie.*"

His sharp tone, such a contradiction to the soft, appeasing voice he's been using, is enough of a surprise to stop me. I turn to face him, my arms crossed tight against my chest.

"You weren't supposed to see it, but that doesn't mean I don't owe you an explanation about it. I do. And that's why I called when I realized I'd left my phone. I know you're mad, and God knows, I'm familiar with your temper. But dammit, I love you."

There's real hurt on his face, and I almost walk toward him. Because right then, I want nothing more than to be wrapped in his arms.

Want it—but can't have it. Not yet. Not until I understand.

So I turn from him and go to the couch. I plop down on it and pull my legs up so that my feet are tucked under me. Then I grab a pillow and hug it. I'm wedged into the corner, fully protected, and yet I feel completely exposed.

"Everything you're saying is bullshit," I tell him, forcing my voice to stay steady. "You know that, right?"

"I asked you to trust me. Now I'm asking you to listen to me. I need to know who you were talking to in the cafe." There's a strange edge to his voice, and I shake my head in confusion.

"I've known her for years," I say. "She found out I was in town, and—"

"I need to find her, Jamie," he says, cutting me off before I can tell him about her fears.

"Why?" Confusion swirls around me. Is Gabby a witness in some sort of case he's been working on? Maybe she's noticed a Stark Security tail and that's what she's afraid of?

"It's important," he says, and it's such a fucking non-answer that I am just seriously done.

"Shouldn't you be looking for your text-happy fuckbuddy instead? Is that why she calls herself F?"

His expression hardens. "I *am* looking for her."

"Well, good. I'm sure you two will be super-duper happy together."

"Goddammit, Jamie. I need—"

"I don't give a fuck what you need. I want to know why my husband is getting texts from skanks. Is this something to do with work? Is she like an informant? Was that a coded message? Because honestly, if the answer to at least one of those questions isn't yes, then I think I better just go to bed. Because if you fucked around on me, Ryan Hunter, I swear to God I'm going to cut your balls off and serve them up to you for breakfast."

He doesn't say a thing, but that doesn't mean the room is silent. On the contrary, it's loud. Full of the sound of pain and blame and fear and loss. And regret. So much regret.

Not Ryan's. *Mine.*

This is Ryan, after all. Hunter. He wouldn't cheat on me. That's not who he is, and I know that. I do.

Don't I?

I close my eyes. *Fuck.*

"Jamie?" His voice is soft and far away. I open my eyes to see him halfway across the room, eyeing me warily. "Do you honestly believe I'd do that? That I'd cheat on you? Hell, that I'd even want to?"

I shake my head, feeling about an inch tall. "No."

I can practically see the relief slide off him. "Good. Because I would never do that."

"I know. I'm sorry—I really am. But you're not telling me anything."

"Christ, I told you I would when—you know what? Never mind. Tell me about the woman in the cafe with you."

"Gabby? What the hell, Ryan? I believe that you aren't sleeping with F-the-bitch-skank, but we are *not* starting another conversation until you tell me what the fuck is going on. Because honestly, you haven't told me shit."

And that's the bottom line. We don't have secrets. Or, okay, we probably do. But the little kind. Like when I said I made him a roast chicken when I only re-heated a roast chicken. He wouldn't care one way or another, but sometimes I want the illusion of being the kind of woman who knows how to do stuff like that for her husband.

And for all I know, Ryan and Damien are secretly watching football and slamming back drinks when they tell me and Nikki that they're working late. And I'd be okay with a secret like that.

I'm not okay with whatever he's not telling me now. Really *not* okay.

His shoulders sag as he exhales. "You know the kind of work I do, Kitten. You know that sometimes I can't tell you everything."

"So this is one of those times? This is a work thing?"

He sighs and cups his hands behind his neck, then goes to sit on the sofa. "I shouldn't," he says. And there's real frustration in his voice. Real pain on the tense, tight features of that gorgeous face.

"Shouldn't? You're the one who left a message saying you'd tell me everything if I just trusted you. Isn't that what you told me?" I still haven't listened to the message. I probably never will.

"Yes, Goddammit. But do you know what kind of risk I'll be taking if I tell you about this? What kind of door I could be opening?"

His voice is slow and controlled. Reasonable. As if I'm making demands on him that I have no right to make.

"No." It takes all my willpower not to shout the word. "I don't know. Because you're not telling me shit. Dammit, Ryan. I trusted you. I trusted you more than anyone in the world. With my body. With my submission. Hell, I trusted you with my dreams. I've told you things I've never told anyone. The good and the bad. *Everything.* And then you actually bring me to this room and talk about trust and submission and love, and all the while there's some bitch out there who's getting off on the memory of you?"

"Jamie—"

"Shut up! Just shut the hell up! You don't trust me enough to tell me what's going on? You fucking bastard!"

A tear runs down my cheek, and I brutally brush it away. I know I sound equal parts angry and needy, stern and confused. I want to pull all my emotions and words back in. I want deniability. To be able to say that no, that wasn't me who was so damn scared and needy.

But I can't help it. Until Hunter, I never had a relationship that didn't end badly. Either the guy left me for someone else, or I got tired and did the leaving.

But Ryan's my life now. He's my everything. And as I stare at him, my mouth dry and my eyes damp, I realize exactly what my problem is— I'm terrified of losing him.

"I can't do this," I whisper, my whole body sagging. "So you tell me now, or I'm moving back to my original room. Because I can't handle any of this."

For a moment, I'm terrified that he'll actually take me up on that. But then he closes his eyes, and seeing the pain on his face is like a reflection of my heart.

He nods, then looks at me. "I'll tell you," he says gently. "But I'm dead serious, Jamie, you can't let on you know. You can't do anything.

You can't say anything. Not to a bellman. Not to Nikki. Not to your goddamn diary."

"I don't keep a diary," I snap, but my words are only for show. He's made his point. "Please, Hunter," I say more gently. "I won't say a word. Just tell me what's going on. Tell me who the hell she is."

His shoulders sink, and he sighs, sounding like Atlas finally easing off the weight of the world. He glances down, speaking more to the floor than to me. "My wife," he says. "I'm pretty sure she's my wife."

Chapter Eight

"Wife?" The word is like Jell-O in my head. It just wobbles around in there, making no sense. Or maybe it's me who's wobbling. I'm shaking, that's for damn sure. And not even with anger. I'm too numb for anger.

Wife?

It's like I'm freezing to death from the inside out. Like I'm dying.

It's shock. It's pain and hurt and betrayal.

It's that feeling you get when someone kicks you so hard you literally fly off the planet and all of the air is sucked out of your lungs and you turn cold and gray and frozen, then just float there in space, the world and everything you love ripped away from you with no warning whatsoever.

It's horrible, and I don't know how to make it stop. I don't even have the energy to try to figure that out.

In front of me, Ryan swallows, then opens his mouth as if to say something. No words come out, though. Instead, he stands, then takes a step toward me, and I shrink back, squeezing my eyes tight as I curl even tighter in on myself, the pillow held close against me.

I'm sure I look as if I'm preparing for a physical blow, trying to shield all my soft spots.

Well, I think, *isn't that what happened? He lashed out. Hit me unexpectedly. My Hunter. The man I love. The man I believed would never, ever hurt me.*

"Jamie." His voice is soft. Sweetly gentle. But I can't look at him. I can't stand knowing that when I open my eyes and point them at him, he's still going to look like the same man he was a few hours ago. The same man I married. The same man I made eggs for back when he was assigned to protect me.

But he's not the same. Not anymore.

"Please. Jamie, I get that you're shocked. But please look at me."

I don't want to—I'm not even sure where I find the strength—but somehow I manage to lift my head.

Slowly, I open my eyes. He's on his knees a few feet away from me, his gorgeous face gray with strain, his eyes dark with pain.

I'm a physical person, no doubt about it. And by pulling away, I've wounded him. But that's just too damn bad. I'm the wronged party here. And this is Jamie time.

"Jamie, Kit—"

He wisely cuts himself off as I tense, a curse forming on my lips.

"Jamie," he repeats. "I'm sorry. You have to believe me. I never expected—"

"*What?* Never expected *what?*" My emotions are like a rollercoaster, and after climbing slowly to the top, I can feel myself going over the curve. I know my temper. So does Ryan. It's going to be one hell of a ride.

I push myself up to a sitting position, my renewed anger fueling me. "Never expected me to find out? Never thought that your other wife might decide she doesn't want to hide in the dark?" I make a scoffing sound. "Oh, yeah. I'll bet you're sorry."

The pain that cuts across his face is like a knife to my soul. "More than I could ever tell you." He moves toward me, walking on his knees like a supplicant. Gingerly, he rests a hand on my thigh, and though I stiffen, I don't flinch away. "I swear on my love for you, I never saw this coming."

I've never seen him this miserable, this unsure. I don't know if he's unsure about me or about the bitch-wife out there in the world.

But maybe it doesn't matter. Because something has shifted. My heart clenches, and a dam breaks inside me. Silent tears streak down my cheeks. "How? How could you not expect a wife to pop up? How could you go our entire relationship without even telling me that you had a wife before me? It doesn't make any sense."

"I know. Oh, Kitten, I know."

This time, I allow the endearment. Hell, maybe I even welcome it. It's an intimate piece of our normal life, and right now, the thing I want most of all is normalcy. Well, normalcy and an explanation.

I straighten my shoulders. "Just tell me. Just spit the whole sordid story out. I can't deal if I don't know, and I think we both know that all the things I'm imagining are probably worse than the reality."

He doesn't agree, which worries me. In fact, for a moment, I think he's going to simply stay quiet. But then he slowly stands. He runs his fingers through his thick, dark hair. His eyes focus beyond me, and when he finally does speak, I realize that he's not even seeing the room. He's gone back into the past. And he doesn't like what he's remembering.

"It was a rescue mission. More than a dozen years ago. I was working security, but I was young enough that I was still a bit green. I was doing work as an independent contractor for an international organization that took on high-risk operations in unsettled countries."

He pauses and I nod to indicate that I understand. And I do. I'm following him completely. I'm just not sure how a wife factors into all of this, and I'm hoping he'll hurry and get to that key part of the story. Especially since he's got some freakish delusion about Gabby folded into the mix.

"Right, well, my boss—Gerard—he got a call from a guy named Randall Cartwright. Old British money. Probably in the line of succession, but definitely up there in British society and industry. He inherited wealth, but he also built his own business, and part of that business involved tech. Communications and weapons. Design and manufacture."

"So he was like Ironman."

"I guess he was," Ryan says, then grins. It's an honest-to-God Ryan grin, and it's a nice moment. We both love the Marvel movies, and we're always first in line at the theater.

"What did this superhero do?"

"He had a daughter. Felicia. A few years younger than me."

"The F from the text message?"

"That's what I'm assuming."

"Assuming? You don't know for sure?"

He runs his fingers through his hair again as he shakes his head. "Kitten, right now, I barely know my own name. All I know for certain is that I love you. Can you trust me long enough to tell this in order? I'll tell you about the text, but let me get there my own way."

"Okay," I say, even though I don't want to wait. But if waiting means that I'll understand, then waiting is what I'll do. I want this past us. I want Ryan.

"Anyway," he continues, "Randall worked with designers and engineers and marketing men from the Middle East. They'd come to the

UK and stay for a few months during product development."

I run all those pieces through my head, then nod, figuring if I don't have it straight, it will all become clear soon. "Go on."

"Apparently Felicia fell for one of those men—a guy named Mikal Safar. And Felicia followed him back home."

"And Daddy was pissed."

"Exactly."

"So far this is an interesting little soap opera, but I'm still not sure how you being married to someone before me fits in."

"I told you. I'm getting there. Okay?"

"Fine. Go on. I just want to get to the part where my husband has another wife."

He ignores my words and my snipey tone. I can't say I blame him.

"Not too long after Felicia followed Mikal, rebels overthrew the government."

"Oh, my God."

He nods, then moves to sit on the couch beside me. He's close enough to touch, but he doesn't reach for me. And I cling tight to my pillow.

"Her father hired Gerard—"

"Your boss, right?"

"Yes. And Gerard sent me. It was supposed to be a simple mission. Get in, find the girl, get out. And it would have been, too, except we didn't know one thing."

I shake my head, wrapped up in the story despite myself.

"Mikal was the son of one of the country's leaders."

"Okay. So?"

"The same day I arrived in the country, Mikal and his father were murdered, and Felicia was on the run."

My mouth drops open but no words come out.

"She was young. Early twenties, and pretty naive. She managed to get a call through to her father, and Gerard got through to me. Suddenly my easy escort job was a full-blown rescue mission, smuggling out the girlfriend of a man the rebels had just executed."

"What did you do?"

"Whatever I could. The first days were chaos, and I managed to get us on a train heading toward the demilitarized zone."

"And you fell in love with her?" My throat is dry as I ask the question. I knew Ryan a long time before we got together, and I know he went out with various women. But I never got the impression that he was serious about anyone. I suppose I projected what I saw in our present into his past.

Still, if there'd been another woman he'd loved, I wish he'd have told me.

"I didn't love her," he says, making me frown.

"Then—oh, shit. Ryan, did she get pregnant? Do you have—"

I can't even say the words. Not that long ago, Nikki and Damien had faced the possibility that Damien had fathered a son. Nikki had dealt, but she'd been twisted up inside. I thought at the time I understood. Now I *really* got it.

"Do I have a child?" His brows rise and there's so much surprise in his voice that I immediately sag with relief.

"You don't. Thank God."

"I married her because it was the only way we had a shot at getting home. We were able to get on that train only because we were married and both from out of the country. And time was of the essence because we knew that soon the rebels would start taking Americans and Brits hostage."

"But didn't they know she'd come with Safar?"

He nods. "The chaos helped. And she worked in her father's business. We said it had been a business trip. Not personal. And we lied and said that I'd been in the country all along doing work of my own."

"So it was just a marriage of convenience?"

He nods.

"So nothing physical?" I remember the words of that text—*our last kiss*—and hope that was all there was.

"We slept together once," he says, shattering that hope. "The night of our wedding. We were both emotional wrecks. We—I guess you could say we needed each other. Jamie," he continues, his voice going low and soft. "I don't regret it. This was a long time before you, and we were both terrified. That night sealed us to each other. And honestly, it added a sheen to our lie. Not only that, but—" He breaks off with a shake of his head.

"What?"

For a moment I don't think he's going to answer. Then he draws in a breath, looks me straight in the eye, and says, "She was a virgin. And, well, considering everything, I didn't regret that night at all. Now, honestly, I don't know what to think."

"Oh." I rub my palms down the soft material of the pillow I'm holding, not sure I understand what he means by that last part.

For that matter, I'm not sure how I feel about any of this.

"At any rate, the bottom line is that what should have been a simple escort scenario turned out to be something out of a goddamn action movie."

"But the idea was that you'd get a divorce when you got back home, right?"

"Absolutely."

"But you didn't." It's a statement, not a question.

"No." I watch as his face turns gray, as if the memories are sucking the life from him. "I didn't think there was a need."

Before I can ask what he means, he continues. "She's dead. Or I thought she was."

"I don't understand."

"To get out, we had to cross a militarized zone by train. The train was attacked. I tried—" His voice breaks. "I tried to protect her. But I failed. It was me against over a dozen men in a raiding party. I ended up with three broken ribs and a bullet in my side. You've seen the scar."

I nod, completely shell-shocked.

"She was killed. Shot in the chest and shoved off the train into a raging river. There was no way she could have survived."

"Ryan, I'm sorry."

The hint of a smile flickers on his lip and he squeezes my hand. I look down, not realizing until then that I'd reached for him.

"I'd failed in the one thing I was supposed to do—protect her. And an innocent woman was dead."

I clutch his hand tighter. "But she's not?"

He hesitates, then moves closer and takes the other hand, too. "Three days ago, I got a text from someone who insisted I meet her at a pub but wouldn't leave her name."

"It was her?"

"Maybe. I got there but the woman was gone. She'd left a note for me. All it said was *I'm sorry.*"

"That she stood you up."

He shakes his head. "Maybe. That's what I thought at first. But I was concerned. Considering my line of work, this woman could be in trouble. Or setting me up. I had Baxter pull footage from nearby cameras."

"And you recognized her? It was Felicia?"

"I always knew I married a smart woman."

I give him a playful smack, but I'm not irritated. I'm scared and a little freaked, but I'm not upset. Not like I was. Now I just want answers. The same ones Ryan wants. "It was her, wasn't it?"

"The video wasn't conclusive, but I saw enough to say for certain that it damn sure looks like the woman I knew."

"The woman you saw die," I say.

"Or not die."

I shiver and tug my hand back, then clutch the pillow again. "She's alive. But how?"

"That's the question. The section of the river the bridge crossed was wild and remote. That's part of what made it such an effective border. No one could survive that fall without help or a miracle, especially not in her condition. If it was a miracle, well, good for her. But if it was help, I don't think it was from a Good Samaritan. Unpopulated and impoverished? Who would have had the ability to get sufficient medical care for her?"

"So what does that mean? No, wait. An extraction."

He almost grins. "See? All those scripts you read and spy movies you watch actually are relevant."

"Well, duh." I grin, too. "Is that honestly what you think?"

"It fits." The ice in his voice matches his eyes, and I know that Hunter is back. "For one thing, it explains how I survived."

"What do you mean?"

"They didn't throw me over. They left me to bleed out, and I got lucky. Why? I always wondered. Now, I think that it wasn't worth the risk of getting me close to the extraction team. I could just as easily die in the train car as in the river. They left me out of an abundance of caution."

"Maybe," I say dubiously.

"Plus, there was always the question of how the rebels got into Mikal's father's complex. It was highly protected. They had to have someone on the inside."

"Felicia? But why?" Immediately, I push the question away. "Actually, I don't care. That's old news and not the problem." I suck in air, fighting back a sob. "What I want to know is why is she back? *Is* she back? You never actually saw her face to face. Maybe someone is pretending to be her. Leaving the note and sending the text. You said the video wasn't actually clear."

The thought perks me up, but Ryan shakes his head, his expression so sad that I can't help but be afraid. Immediately, my world starts to crumple again. "What?" I demand. "What do you know?"

"I need you to listen to me, Jamie. No, no, I don't care if you listen or not. What I need you to do is obey. Can you do that, Kitten? Without a collar—in real life—can you do what I say without question?"

"I—" I swallow, then lick my lips. "Ryan, you're scaring me."

"Good," he says. "If you're scared, maybe you'll do what I say."

"I don't—"

"Go home, Jamie. Go home and stay with Nikki and Damien. Or go to New York and stay with Dallas and Jane. Their place is a damn fortress."

I wince. Our friend Dallas used to head up a vigilante organization that rescued kidnap victims and other innocents in situations where official channels didn't work. He has enemies. Lots. And the house really is secure. But it's a long way from our home in LA and a long way from here. And I don't understand why he wants me gone.

Slowly, I shake my head. "What's going on? Come on, Hunter, talk to me. Why do you want to send me away?"

"For Christ's sake, Jamie, I want to keep you safe." The words burst out of him, their force launching him to his feet. He paces in front of the couch, and I simply watch him, not understanding why he's so concerned about me.

"You think because we're married she's going to try to take me out or something?"

"If she's alive, then I think there's a good chance she's in intelligence—or that she was all those years ago. And that she was working with the dissidents. If she's popping up now, there must be a good reason. Something she needs desperately—apparently from me. Something she will do anything to get. Including leveraging my wife."

I swallow. "Like what?"

"Kitten, I don't know. But I don't think it's because she wants me to help her book a suite at one of Damien's hotels."

"No. Probably not. Wow." I grew up in Dallas with dreams of becoming a movie star. And though I've watched a lot of spy movies, I never truly touched upon the world of spies and intelligence and security until I met Ryan. For that matter, I hadn't touched upon much of anything until I moved to Los Angeles and my best friend got involved with Ryan's boss, Damien Stark. You see a lot of interesting things when your bff gets involved with a billionaire. But never once in all the years since I started living in the Stark orbit did I think that I would somehow end up inside some sort of bizarre espionage plot.

I frown. "Leverage me," I repeat. "But—but she doesn't even know I exist."

"She does," he says. "And she's already shown me that she can get to you in a heartbeat."

I gape at him. I don't have a clue what he's talking about.

He sits beside me, then takes my hands. "Kitten, I need you to answer my question."

I blink, completely confused. "What ques—?"

"The cafe, Kitten. Who were you with in the cafe?"

"Gabby? She's a friend from college. What does she have to—" I sit up straighter, then shake my head. "Oh, no. No. That's crazy."

"Maybe it is," he says. "But there are only two things in this world I trust with absolute certainty. You. And my own two eyes. That's her, baby. The woman in the cafe is Felicia."

Chapter Nine

"Gabby?" Jamie shook her head. "No. Ryan, that's impossible."

"Is it?" He sat next to her, then took her hand. "Because, honestly, I'd be thrilled to know that she's not really Felicia." So would Jamie, he thought. And not just because such proof would mean that Gabby wasn't a liar at best and a spy at worst. But also because of the rest of it.

The worst of it.

But Jamie hadn't gotten there yet, and he didn't intend to push her. She was still numb, but she'd see the horrible truth soon enough. Right now, they just needed to go over the facts.

And maybe—just maybe—it would turn out that Jamie was right. Maybe there was no way that Gabby could be Felicia. Maybe the texts were a hoax. Maybe there was nothing at all to worry about.

He hoped that was the case. But he knew in his gut that it wasn't. Even so, he nodded. "All right. Tell me the story. Why can't she be Felicia?"

"Because I've known her for years. And she's not British. You said Felicia was British, right?"

He nodded.

"See?"

"Kitten, it's not that hard to hide an accent. You tell me that yourself every time we watch a movie with a British actor playing an American."

She made a face. "Okay, fine. What about school? She went to the University of Texas with Nikki and me."

"She's your age?" A tiny bit of hope bloomed in him. Felicia would be older than Jamie. Of course, if she'd changed her identity, she'd likely be lying about her age, too.

Jamie shook her head. "A few years older. She was a grad student finishing up her masters when Nikki and I were freshmen. She had the apartment above us. We used to hang out at the pool. Drink. That kind of thing."

"When was this? What year?"

She told him, and he nodded, that tiny bloom of hope starting to open. "That's after the mission, but you said she was a grad student. That means she'd been there at least a year doing graduate work and then four years before, right? As an undergrad?" If she'd been in school in Texas during the mission, she hardly could have been in the Middle East with him.

"I—" Her shoulders slumped, and he knew the answer. "Well, no, actually. She'd only come for one semester because of the collection of medieval texts that UT has. Her field was history. The Middle Ages. She didn't go to UT undergrad."

"Where did she go?"

Jamie's brow furrowed. "I don't remember. Somewhere in New York, I think."

The hope withered and died. "I'm sorry, Kitten, but don't you see? After her extraction, she went under. She got a new life. The history degree. College. All of that was about building a new life. A new identity."

"No," Jamie said, but he could tell her heart wasn't in it. "No, it doesn't make sense. She's my friend. And now it turns out she's your ex-wife? That's too crazy to believe."

"The world is full of crazy coincidences, Kitten."

"But why get in touch with me? She told me how she tracked me down. Nikki married Damien, so of course she saw pictures. And she saw me, too. Lots of Hollywood stuff, right? And she paid attention and learned who I was married to, and—*oh.*"

Her eyes filled with fear. "Ryan, she saw that I was married to you. And she knew that if anyone could help her, you could."

"Help her?"

"There's something wrong. Seriously wrong. She's scared, but she didn't tell me why. Running from someone, maybe. And she's been reaching out to you all along. Hunter, you've got to help her."

He sat back, trying to process that. "That makes no sense. I showed up both times, and she wasn't there. And when I saw her with you at the cafe, she bolted. That doesn't sound like someone who wants my help.

Just the opposite, in fact."

Her brow furrowed. "Maybe. Or maybe it sounds like someone who screwed you over, and now she's afraid you know." She cocked her head. "Hunter, do you think maybe she is on the run?"

"I don't know. If she really was in intelligence, I wouldn't be surprised."

"Maybe she thinks you're after her."

"Maybe she does." If she believed that he'd figured out her ruse and would expose her, then it made sense. Except that Felicia had been off his radar for years. Why now?

"I don't know," Jamie said after he'd voiced the question to her. "I get that maybe she's not the girl I knew in college—I do. And if everything you've said is true—if she did help murder that man and pull off that coup—then she's nothing like I thought she was. But I can't wrap my head around it. Honestly, I can't get my mind around any of it. Imagine living a lie all this time. Being alive when the whole world thinks you're dead. That would be—"

She cut off her words mid-thought, her eyes going wide as she tilted her head up and looked at him.

He'd expected it, this look of understanding. This final punch in the gut. But even having anticipated it, the expression on her face still ripped his soul to shreds.

"You didn't divorce her," she whispered. "You didn't get a divorce because you didn't have to. Because you don't have to divorce a dead wife."

"No," he said simply. "You don't."

"But she's not dead. If Gabby is Felicia, then she's not dead."

"No. No, she isn't."

Her throat moved as she swallowed. "Then you're still married to her." Her forehead creased, her expression shifting into a mask of hurt and betrayal. "And, oh God, Ryan. That means I'm not your wife."

"No." The word burst out of him. "The hell you're not." Raw fury burned in his voice. "You're my everything, Jamie. It's only ever been you. Whatever is going on, we will figure it out. We will solve it, and we will fix it. You're my wife. For now, for always."

"I believe you." He could see that she was fighting tears, trying to be calm. Practical. "But Hunter, you can only have one wife. And the first one wins the toss." She bit her lower lip, thinking. "Except everyone thought she was dead, right? Maybe there's a death certificate?"

"There probably is." He knew that he'd taken the news back to Randall—hell, he'd told Randall everything that happened on the mission—and Randall would have taken care of all the legal details surrounding her death.

"But she's not dead now, Hunter. So what does that mean? Legally, about us?"

"I don't know, Kitten. I wish I did."

She lifted haunted eyes to him, and he died a little bit. He'd done this to her. Hurt her so damn deeply. And even though he knew it wasn't his fault—knew that he'd had no reason to expect Felicia's return from the dead—he still wanted to put his fist through a goddamn wall.

"Jamie. Kitten. Talk to me. Do you want a blanket? Some wine?"

She shook her head, then nodded. "Yes. I mean no. Fuck wine. I want whiskey. A double shot of whiskey. And after that I want another."

He almost smiled. That, at least, was a spark of the woman he knew.

"I'll be right back." The bar wasn't far away, and he watched her as he poured them both a double, neat.

"We have to find out the truth," Jamie said when he returned with the drinks. "If she's in danger, I want to help. And if it's the opposite…well, as much as I hate the thought that Gabby's been playing with me, it would be worse if it turns out she's a danger to you."

He nodded. If she'd come in from the cold, there must have been a reason. And as he was one of the few people who knew her before, he was a liability.

But if she intended to kill him, why not take advantage of the earlier opportunities? Too public? No nerve? Sentimentality?

It all curled back to the basics. Until they knew the truth, they'd never find answers. And they needed answers to get to the truth.

"Shoot her a text," he told Jamie. "Tell her we're both worried. Tell her we want to help her."

"Okay. But just for the record, I'm not going back. I'm staying right here with you."

He couldn't hide his smile. "Kitten, I know."

"What are you going to do?"

"I'm going to get Baxter on her trail, and then I'll text her the same damn thing. And hope to hell she believes me."

She finished the text and put her phone on the table, then took a long swallow of whiskey. "No reply yet."

"I'm not surprised. Either she's Felicia and she's determined to avoid both of us now since you know the score, or she's Gabby and she's in danger and thinking it over first."

"Do you think that's possible?"

"Hell, I don't know. She looks a hell of a lot like her. But it's been a lot of years." Even so, he trusted his instinct. But it was going to crush Jamie if it turned out her friend had lied to her all along. And if it turned out that the friend wanted Ryan out of the way? Well, that was a hell that he didn't want Jamie to suffer until they were damn certain of the truth.

"I'm sorry," she whispered, scooting closer and twining her fingers with his.

His brow furrowed. "Sorry? Sorry for what?"

She shrugged. "I don't even know." A tiny choked sob escaped with a burst of laughter. "For melting down, I guess. And," she added as she gave his hand a quick squeeze, "for not trusting you."

She looked him right in the eyes as she spoke, and the sincere regret he saw in her face just about melted him.

"You trusted me, Kitten. You always have and you always will. Do you think I don't know that?"

One shoulder rose and fell. "I doubted you, Hunter. I really did. And I hate myself for it."

"No," he said firmly. "You don't have a thing to apologize for. You were jealous and confused, and that's on me. I should have called and told you the moment I recognized her in the video feed. I didn't, and," he added with a hint of a smile, "I deserved every lash that well-honed temper of yours doled out. Okay?"

"Thank you."

"For what?"

A tear snaked down her cheek. "For always getting me."

"Well, Kitten, it's been a long course of study. But I do enjoy getting educated."

She started to laugh, but he silenced her with a kiss, relishing the taste of Jamie mixed with whiskey. A familiar taste and one he never tired of.

He started the kiss slow, but it didn't stay that way. His wife was responsive as hell and always had been. Her lips parted in a silent demand that he kiss her harder. At the same time, her fingers curled around the back of his neck, pulling him closer in an equally strong demand that he deepen their kiss. Their connection.

She squirmed on the couch, her soft moans shooting straight to his cock, and all he wanted in that moment was to claim her. To take her right there. To hold her hair as she sucked him off, then take her hard and fast as she screamed his name.

He wanted to own her. He wanted to do every dirty thing he could think of to her, just to prove she was his. Just for the joy of knowing that she would obey. More than that, that she wanted to.

But he couldn't. Not now. Not tonight.

She deserved sweet kisses and soft caresses. And he wanted to show her how much he loved her. How much he cherished her.

She was his life, his love, and he'd brought her pain today. Not intentionally, but that didn't matter. Tonight, he was going to hold back on his urge to claim her.

Tonight, he was simply going to make love to his wife.

Chapter Ten

"With me," Ryan says as he stands, holding out a hand for me. I take it and follow, eager for whatever he has in mind. He pauses at the foot of the bed, then lets his gaze roam over me. He comes closer, then takes the hem of my T-shirt and starts to pull it up. "You, Kitten, are wearing far too many clothes."

"No argument from me," I say, my finger going to the buttons on my jeans. I shimmy out of them, taking my panties too. Then I kick them free of my feet and stand there, hyperaware of my body as I wait for Ryan to tell me what to do.

"You're so fucking beautiful," he says, then urges me onto the bed with him. I follow, then suck in air as his tongue teases my nipple before he closes his mouth over my breast and gently sucks while his fingertips caress the curve of my waist.

It's sweet and loving and tender—and it's not at all what I want.

I squirm a little, hoping he'll slide his hand down to my cunt and finger fuck me hard or tease my ass or even bite my nipple. I want to feel electricity tingle inside me. I want to be on fire.

I want him to do every dirty thing we've ever done and then some. Because as wonderful as making love with my husband can be, right now, I need to be taken. Fucked.

I need to be owned, and while I know I should just tell Ryan that, what I want is for *him* to know it. To understand me the way that he always has before.

I know why I want it—other than the fact that I will always, eagerly submit to Ryan. But this is more than that. I get that it's because of Felicia. I know that some part of me is fighting in protest against the thought that there's ever been another woman, much less a wife.

His hands still roam my body, and he claims my mouth in a gentle kiss. It's tender, loving, and I moan with genuine pleasure as his lips trail kisses down my neck. I'm turned on—hell, yes, I am—but I want more. Need more. And I pull gently away and meet his eyes.

For a moment, we only look at each other. Then I feel something shift. A change in the air. In the temperature of the room. There's heat now. Electricity.

"Hunter," I say, but he interrupts me.

"No. I talk. You do what I say. Understood?"

God, yes. I almost come right then. Instead, I say, very clearly, "Yes, Sir."

I'm practically giddy with relief. *He knows.* Somehow he always knows exactly what I need.

He gets off the bed, leaving me on the mattress. He's still in his suit, and now he takes his jacket off along with his tie. He tosses the jacket over a chair, but the tie he keeps in his hands. "Lean back, Kitten. Hands on the mattress. That's my girl," he says when I comply. "Now spread your knees and put the soles of your feet together."

I do, feeling the incredible stretch in my inner thighs. And the heat of my pussy, fully exposed to him.

"Beautiful," he murmurs. "And wet," he adds, easily sliding two fingers into me as if to prove the point.

"What toys did you bring?" he asks, and my whole body responds from nothing more than the tone in his voice.

"I—toys?"

He chuckles, then slides me closer to the end of the mattress so that my toes are just peeking over.

"Toys," he repeats, getting on his knees, then tugging me forward until my cunt is right over his mouth. His tongue laves me as his hands hold my thighs open, keeping me firmly in place.

"I know you, Kitten," he whispers between lashes of his tongue. "Tell me where they are and I'll look for myself."

"Don't you have any here?"

"For all the other women I fuck?" He kisses the inside of my thighs, the stubble of his beard on my sensitive skin feeling amazing. "Is that what you're telling me? Do you want to watch me touch another woman?"

I shake my head. "No." There was a time when watching a guy with another woman would have turned me on. But not now. Not with Ryan. With him, I don't share. "Never," I say.

It occurs to me that if he really wants to push the envelope—wants to prove just how thoroughly he owns me—he could bring in another man to fuck me while he watches. "You don't...?"

"I don't," Ryan says, obviously reading my mind. "But what humbles me is knowing that you would if I wanted it. Wouldn't you?"

I nod. Because God help me, if that's what he wanted, I would. But I don't want to. I don't want anyone's touch but Ryan's.

"Good girl." He rewards me with a kiss, and his fingers slide inside me. Greedily, I hump his hand, feeling like I truly have been a good girl, but all too soon he pulls his fingers free, leaving me hot and needy and longing to be fucked, teased, spanked, everything. Right now, I'm nothing but need, and I want to melt into Ryan's arms and let him use me to satisfy every one of his wicked cravings.

"Come on, Kitten. Tell me. Where are they?"

"Pink rolling bag," I concede, shooting him a grimace when he chuckles.

He takes the tie that he's been holding and secures it over my eyes. I consider telling him I have a blindfold in the bag but decide I should keep my mouth closed. Then he tells me to stand.

I comply, of course, my legs slightly apart, just like he ordered, and my arms at my sides.

"Now wait," he says, and soon I hear the familiar sound of the suitcase's zipper and the shifting of my various packing cubes until, finally, he returns.

"Eyes stay closed," he says, his fingers gently stroking my left nipple, then squeezing so hard I gasp. Then I gasp again when his fingers are replaced by metal nipple clamps. "Lovely idea," he says once he's clamped both my nipples. "Can you feel it, Kitten? The sensation spreading all the way from your tits to that gorgeous pussy?"

I nod.

"Tell me what it feels like."

"Electricity. Heat. Like a live wire burning inside me. It makes me want more. Everything."

"Everything?"

"I want to be touched. I want to be fucked. Hunter, please."

"Soon. Turn around, then walk two steps. You'll hit the bed."

I do, and he's right.

"Now bend over so that you're right up against the mattress. I want your pretty pussy rubbing the spread every time I spank you." I comply, and since the bed is tall, I'm essentially bent over at the waist in a perfect right angle.

My core clenches, my body so close to exploding I'm sure I would come if he just kept talking. He's going to spank me, of course, and my senses are on overdrive in anticipation of Hunter's touch.

"Christ that's lovely. Do you know how hard it makes me seeing you bent over like that? Waiting for me to take you? To fuck you? Do you know how much you humble me, Kitten? Have you got any idea what it means to me knowing that you'll give yourself this way? Knowing that you belong to me?"

"Always," I say. "I'm yours, Hunter. You know I am."

"I do," he says, gently rubbing the swell of my ass. "It's the greatest miracle of my life, finding you. Loving you. Claiming you."

"Claim me now," I whisper. "I love you, too, but right now, please, just fuck me hard."

He chuckles. "That's my Kitten," he says, and his words are followed almost immediately by a sharp, unexpected smack to my ass.

I gasp at the red-hot sensation, then sigh with pleasure as it seems to spread out, the tingling redness, the naughty sting. It's a special kind of claiming, I think. He's marking me, and I'm giving myself to him.

Gently, he rubs over the sore area until the pain has faded to a dull ache. Then he issues another demand. "Spread your legs," he orders, and though I want him to slip his fingers between my thighs and caress my pussy, he doesn't. Instead he says, "There's only you, Kitten. There's only ever been you. And for the record, I will kill any man who touches you. So, no. There will be no sharing of my wife."

"Thank goodness," I say, then yelp as another smack lands on my ass, making my cunt clench in pleasure. I want him inside me desperately, but mostly I'm just happy that he's claiming me.

One more smack, and my body jolts on the bed, the combination of the sting and the tug on the clamps as my body moves making my skin tingle with a wild desire. Then I start to melt when his hand soothes the sting before sliding once again between my legs. I'm incredibly wet, and this time, he takes full advantage, thrusting his fingers deep inside me. His body arches over mine, his slacks rubbing my ass as his tongue teases my ear. "Do you want me to fuck you?"

"Yes. God, yes."

"Not just yet." Instead, I hear him move to get something else. A moment later, he's back, stroking my ass, and then I feel the cool, slick lube followed by the pressure of the bulbous head of a butt plug. I relax, giving in to the spectacular sensation of the glass bulb filling me.

He sucks in a sharp breath. "I love this ass. One of the few perfect asses in the world, I think. And so very pretty with this little pink flower." He presses down on the plug, and I moan with pleasure. Then, without warning, he spanks me again, and the impact on my ass coupled with the pressure of the plug is so fucking extraordinary I actually cry out, my whole body shaking. Moisture slides down my thighs, and all I want—*all I want*—is Ryan's cock inside me.

"Please," I beg, my whole being lost in a sensual haze.

He says nothing but soothes the spot, then finger fucks me, moving in and out with such intensity that I imagine it's his cock pounding me toward heaven, and I hear myself crying, "yes, yes," from the intense pleasure of it all.

I'm just about to beg again when I feel him behind me. The brush of material from his slacks. The hard heat of his cock. I bite my lower lip, relishing this. Knowing that he's still dressed and I'm not only naked but blindfolded and plugged.

I'm his. I belong to him. His wife. His lover. His everything.

When he thrusts his cock inside me, I cry out his name, letting myself get lost in the sensation of being completely filled and thoroughly fucked.

My tits and clit are rubbing the bedspread as Ryan's cock does a number on that sweet spot deep inside me. I'd love to just stay like this forever, but I don't even own my own pleasure anymore. I've handed it over to Ryan, and he's toying with me. Taking me higher and higher only to pull back until finally I feel the tremor in his body and I know that his release is close. And as he starts to shatter, he whispers one last demand of me.

"Come," he says.

And God help me, my body obeys, bursting apart at the seams in an explosion of pleasure and sensation, lust and love, hope and happiness.

And Ryan, I think as I fall back to earth, sucked down by an overwhelming need for sleep.

Always, Ryan.

Chapter Eleven

I wake sated and happy, my body pressed close to Ryan's. For a moment, I simply lie there soaking up his comfort, feeling warm and loved and safe.

Safe.

Reality hits me, and I scramble across the ocean of a bed for my side table. Beside me, Ryan mumbles something unintelligible, then rolls over, hogging the covers as usual.

I grab my phone, hoping Gabby's reply from last night is waiting for me, but there's nothing in my texts except for one from Nikki reminding me to call and tell her how The Plan fared. Too bad I promised Ryan not to say anything to her.

"Did she text?" Ryan asks, and I roll back over to find him watching me, looking sleepily sexy. I shake my head, then reach out to rub my palm over his jaw, now more stubbly than it was last night when it rubbed provocatively against my inner thigh.

"Mmm," I say, and see a corresponding hunger in his eyes. "Can we pretend it's still night and stay in bed?"

"Kitten, I don't need the night as an excuse with you. But," he adds, taking my hand from his cheek so that he can kiss my palm, "I should check my phones, too. And make sure there's nothing that needs my immediate attention at work. Then I should probably pay a visit to her family."

"Her dad? He's the one who hired you to go get her, right?"

"He's passed away," Ryan tells me. "But she has an uncle. I want to feel him out. See if she's been in contact with him."

"If she hasn't, are you going to tell him that she might be back?"

He shakes his head. "No. Why get his hopes up? But he needs to know there's someone out there claiming to be her. If it's really Felicia, he'll learn soon enough."

"Makes sense," I say, sliding off the bed to head into the bathroom. When I come back out, he's already dressed, and I pout. "That's what I get for letting you shower last night. Think of the morning we could have had."

"I'm already thinking of it," he says, with that rough edge to his voice that I know so well. The one that makes my pussy purr.

I bite my lip and take a step toward him, still totally naked. "What are you thinking?"

He reaches out, his thumbs and forefingers closing over both my still-tender nipples, tight enough that I wince as I settle into the pain.

"You like that," he says as he tugs me toward him, and sparks ricochet inside me.

"Yes," I say, now only inches from him and glowing in anticipation.

"So do I." He releases me, then uses one fingertip to trace around my areola before snaking down lower. He pauses at my navel, then goes lower still, until his fingertip finds my clit, then slips between my slick folds.

I bite down harder, forcing myself not to react. But when he raises that same finger to my lips and tells me to suck, I just about lose it. "Hunter, please."

That's all I can manage. I'm lost in a forest of need, and he's my only way out.

"That's my girl." He nods toward the bed again. "There. Face down, arms and legs spread. Now."

I nod, then move obediently onto the bed, positioning myself as he asked—facedown and spread wide. I make a low, needy sound, then sigh with pleasure as the mattress shifts with his weight when he sits beside me, his hand on my back.

"I want you like this when I get back," he says, and I immediately stiffen. "Like this, and I'll give you everything you want. Every pleasure imaginable, every delicious fantasy. I'll make you come again and again," he whispers, sliding his hand over my ass. "But it will be a reward for obeying me. For belonging to me."

"So tell me, Kitten," he continues. "Will you wait like this? Will you do as I say? Will you wait like this?"

"Yes," I say, because this is Ryan, and he knows me. He understands that I need this time to calm down. To settle into myself.

More than that, I know that he needs it, too. The knowledge that I'll obey. That I'll wait and think and drift and process. Because I will. And by doing so, when he returns, I'll have earned every decadent thing that he's promising.

* * * *

I'm not sure how long I stay like that, facedown on the bed, my legs spread and my body open and yearning. All I know is that the worry and fear that had been plaguing me begins to drift away. I know—I've always known—that Ryan loves me. That he wants me. And that there is no other woman but me for him.

That certainty warms me, filling me with a desperate longing. I want to feel his large hands upon me. His breath on the back of my neck. The pressure of his body against my rear as he enters me from behind or fucks me in the ass.

I shiver, and it's only with a stern mental command that I manage to keep my hands spread as ordered. On the contrary, I'm having a hell of a time resisting the urge to let my fingertips trail along the duvet until I find the sensitive skin at my waist. I want to slide my fingers beneath my own body and gently stroke my clit, letting the pressure build along with my fantasies.

That, however, is forbidden. Ryan said so. And though he's not here with me, I won't disobey. At least, not in reality. In my fantasies, all bets are off, and I let my mind drift, imagining the feel of my own fingers on my body. Losing myself in the erotic pleasure of my pretend touch as I wait for the real strength of my husband's hands.

I'm not sure how long I stay like that, but I must have drifted off. Because I'm startled back to reality by the click of a lock and the light thump of footsteps on the plush carpet. I want to roll over and open my eyes. I want to see Ryan—tall and lean, his expression hard even as his blue eyes darken with passion—and yet that is against the rules, too.

So I remain as I am. My eyes closed, but my body tingling. Aware. Waiting.

I feel the shift of the bed, and though I'm expecting a gentle caress, I can't deny the flood of warmth to my clit as something hard and flat smacks me once across the ass, leaving a sting and then a pleasant numbness. I feel a sharp twinge—like a pulled muscle in my glute—as I spread my legs wider, gnawing on my lower lip so that I won't cry out or moan with pleasure. That, of course, is my part of this game.

Then I feel the dance of fingertips over my lower back and up my spine. My hair, which these days reaches my shoulder blades, is brushed aside, and there is a gentle pressure as his hand cups my neck.

There's something odd about his touch, though I'm not sure what. I can't wrap my mind around it, mostly because I can't wrap my mind around anything. I'm floating now, my mind untethered. I feel as if I've drunk an entire bottle of wine after hiking ten miles. And I'm tired. So very, very tired…

He's not touching me now, but I know that he will soon, and I don't want to drift off. And yet I can't seem to hold on to reality. I can't even open my eyes—I'm not supposed to; I know that. And yet I try. I have to. But it's not possible. I'm too tired, to drained, too damn sleepy.

And though I want to revel in the feel of Ryan's touch, I simply don't have the strength. Instead, I give in to the sweet pull of slumber and let the warm waves of dreams carry me away…

Chapter Twelve

"William Atkinson," Ryan said, speaking into his headset as he exited the elevator. "Felicia's uncle. I need an address." He'd just left Jamie in the suite—and the view of her laid out naked on the bed for him, her body flush with desire—had painted what felt like a permanent smile on his face, despite the dicey circumstances swirling around them. Now, though, he'd thoroughly shifted gears. And the sooner he did the work, the sooner he could get back to his wife.

"Sure," Baxter said on the other end of the line. "One second." It took closer to fifteen seconds, but then Baxter rattled it off. "It was Randall's house in Kensington. I can't see all the information without going deeper—that would take some time—but looks like he's renting it. I would have thought he'd inherit."

"Probably a tax thing," Ryan said, thinking of all the holding companies his friend Damien had set up over the years.

He crossed the lobby, then stepped outside and signaled for the valet to call a taxi as Baxter continued. "Looks like there's nobody else with an interest in the property." His voice on the call crackled slightly as Ryan stepped up to the approaching cab. "Did Randall have any other family?"

"Just Felicia," Ryan said as he settled in the backseat. "And William's his stepbrother, by the way. About fifteen years older if I remember right. Their mother had William when she was a teen. She married Randall's father—his name's Harold—in her mid-twenties when William was about ten. She died when William was at university. A riding accident, I think."

Felicia had told him the story during their escape. By that time, he'd heard most of it already. He'd gone on the mission knowing he might have to pose as her husband or fiancé, and it made sense to know as much about her and her family as possible.

"I don't think Harold ever considered William his son. I know Harold left the entire estate—and it was massive—to Randall."

"Ouch."

"That's what I thought. But Felicia said her uncle was cool about it. He didn't like Harold and didn't want his hand-me-downs. She adored him. Which is why I want to let him know some of what's going on."

"And try to find out if he has any information on where she is, what she's up to, or if she was ever even dead."

"Sharp man," Ryan said. "And that's why I hired you."

Baxter laughed, and they ended the call just as the cab pulled out onto the street. He gave the driver the address, then got back on his phone, this time responding to the text from Gabby or whoever the hell had been contacting him. She hadn't answered last night, and he didn't expect an answer now, but he was going to damn well keep trying.

I'm alone and can talk. Worried about you. Why are you running from me?

He closed the app and started checking his emails, relieved to see that there were still no crises brewing and his staff was handling the system upgrade beautifully.

He was responding to a question about a server upgrade when a text flashed over the top of his screen—*Does Jamie know?*

He frowned. Did she mean did Jamie know that he'd been married? Or did Jamie know that Gabby was Felicia? He didn't know and settled on a noncommittal response.

She's worried about you.

He waited, the phone tight in his hand, but no response came. Another block, another turn. Still nothing.

Felicia. Are you there?

A moment. Then…

I'm here.

Ryan drew in a breath, then opened his text thread with Baxter. He quickly tapped out the situation, gave Baxter the new number she was texting from, and mentally crossed his fingers.

Tell me what you need. Tell me why you reached out to me, only to run from me.

I'm scared.

Of me?

I don't know.

Ryan started to answer, but before he finished, another message popped up.

I want to talk. Public. Your hotel. I'll sit at the bar. We can move to a table, but only if there are other people near us.

Fine.

Now?

He hesitated. *Not there now but can cancel plans and come back.*

He waited for her to answer, hoping she hadn't changed her mind.

Thirty long seconds passed, and he couldn't stand it anymore. *Felicia?*

One. I'll be there at one.

He considered that. He hadn't intended to leave Jamie that long, but it was still less time than he'd left her in the past. It had started almost as a game—leaving her so she could calm down and get centered. But it had become much more.

Alright. I'll see you at one.

I'm tossing this phone. I'll have another new number when you see me.

That didn't surprise him.

Okay. See you then.

But there was no answer. Apparently, she'd already tossed the phone.

Immediately, he called Baxter. "Did you get her location?"

"You won't believe it."

"I think I will. Is she near the hotel?"

"That she is," Baxter says. "Or was when we pinged her."

Using a Type-O or "Silent" SMS, Baxter had essentially pinged her phone to capture her location. Then he'd used Stark Security's various resources to triangulate a location. Unfortunately, it wasn't exact, which meant it would take some time to find the phone she'd ditched, but Ryan was certain Baxter and his team were up to the task.

"She won't be there now," Ryan said. "But she tossed her phone. Get a team to find it."

"On it," Baxter said. "We'll start with the public trashcans near the hotel and work our way out. I doubt she was in the lobby. That would be a little too ballsy."

"Contact me when you have the phone," Ryan said. "Let's see what we can get off her SIM card. And get the IT team to hack her password."

"Will do. By the way, I did a quick search on William. His first wife died not long after Felicia disappeared. He went on a drinking binge, ended up marrying a woman named Carolyn Grey. Old money family that's been living on credit for at least a generation. It's her second marriage, and she's got a son, Patrick. He's a doctor who lives in Belgium But Carolyn and William don't have any children together."

"Thanks. I just got to William's house. I'll call when I'm free for ar update."

"You got it, boss," Baxter said, then clicked off.

Ryan paid the driver, then slipped out of the cab and stood for a moment on the sidewalk outside the majestic property. He guessed that the grandiose home had been built in the mid-nineteenth century. It stil stood tall and proud, but it had become a bit shabby around the edges The gardens weren't quite tended. The paint wasn't quite fresh. A few weeds peeked up between the stones leading to the front door, and the polish on the wood of the foreboding entrance seemed dull and lackluster

Still, the grounds were clean, and when the maid ushered him in, he saw that the interior was tidy. But it, too, had an air of neglect, as if the overwhelming home was simply too much for the occupants.

Perhaps Randall hadn't left the property to William. Maybe he'd left it to someone else, or even to his own corporation, and William was simply a renter. But even so, why not do a better job maintaining such a stunning residence?

An interesting question, but not one he spent much time pondering How the Cartwright and Atkinson families lived wasn't his concern. He was there only to update William on the mystery surrounding his niece.

"I'm sorry, sir," the maid said the moment she opened the door "Mrs. Atkinson is out."

"I actually need to speak to Mr. Atkinson, if he's available. I'm a friend of his late niece."

"Oh. I see. One moment." She was the picture of polite efficiency but Ryan couldn't help but think that there was something awkward about her manner. As if this wasn't a request she fielded often, if at all.

She disappeared but returned soon enough, asking him to follow The rest of the interior bolstered his impression of the exterior. The place was only minimally maintained. The staff kept it clean, but there was stil the sense that the mansion was only biding its time. Basically, the place needed some good old-fashioned TLC.

They entered the library, the first room he'd seen that appeared to be regularly cleaned and maintained. But despite the polished floors and dust-free shelves and fixtures, the room had a musty, pungent smell. *Old books*, Ryan thought. And something else. Something less pleasant than the comfortable scent of paper and glue and ink. *Hospital.* That was it, he realized. The room had the underlying stench of death.

As he looked toward the far corner of the room, he saw why. An elderly man sat in a dark corner in a huge leather recliner, a heavy walking stick propped within arm's length. A dark blanket covered most of his body, but the eyes behind his glasses were alert as he lifted a pen and signaled to Ryan.

"Who the hell are you?" The voice held unexpected strength and humor.

"Ryan Hunter. I knew your niece, Felicia."

He waved his hand. "Come where I can see you. And *you*, you stay over there."

Ryan turned to see that the maid was still in the room. Now she settled into a chair in the corner. She reached into a basket at her feet and began to knit. Apparently, she spent a lot of time in that corner, and Ryan presumed that she was more nurse than maid these days.

As ordered, he stepped closer, and as his eyes adjusted, he saw that William looked older than his seventy-six years. A man who'd been worn down by more than just time.

"You did a bit more than know her," William said, and the small smile alone seemed to make him stronger. "The way Randall told me, you married her. Tried to save her."

"I did. I didn't realize Mr. Cartwright had told you. The circumstances were...odd."

William chuckled. "They were indeed. That girl was always getting into odd situations. Adored that little thing. Special. That's what she was. Couldn't have loved her more if she'd been my own blood grandchild. Hell, I couldn't have loved her more if there'd been two of her."

"She was special, yes. But sir, I was hoping to ask you—"

"Poppycock!"

Ryan straightened. "I'm sorry?"

"No, no. Not no." He tapped the end of the pen on a flimsy paper book in his lap. "The puzzle. Crossword. This one's been a mighty bugger, but I finally conquered it." He closed the book, then held it out. "Well, come here."

Ryan came, then took the book that the man extended. "Ah, shall I toss it?"

"Heavens no." He lowered his voice. "Been doing crosswords all my life. Always save the books." He spoke with the seriousness of someone revealing state secrets.

William gestured to a shelf stacked with magazines and other books and Ryan added the latest completed book of crosswords to the pile.

"Bring me a fresh book," William said. "Then tell me why you're here. Something about my house in Somerset, wasn't it? I do miss the country life."

"Actually, I'm trying to learn the name of an attorney that Randall had retained for some private affairs. Did he ever mention the lawyer to you?"

William made a *phht* noise. "I wasn't involved in the business. Hate lawyers. Damn snakes. I saw a python once. Marvelous creature."

Ryan drew in a breath. "They are. Yes." He cleared his throat. "Actually, I'm concerned that someone may be impersonating Felicia," Ryan said as he handed him the new book.

"What? Now?" William opened the book and started scribbling in answers.

"Yes, sir. Has anyone contacted you suggesting that your niece is alive? Or suggesting that she is your niece?"

The man peered at him. "Why would they?"

"Sometimes people do odd things." He was glad to know Felicia hadn't been gaslighting her uncle, but that only doubled down on the question of what her endgame was.

"Deadlocked."

"I'm sorry?"

"The word, the word." He tapped the pen. "Pay attention, boy. A four-letter word for deadlocked."

"Ah, even?"

William pointed the pen at him. "Clever. I do imagine she's nearby sometimes." He sighed. "The regrets of an old man, I suppose. I used to enjoy talking with her. Had a good head on her shoulders." He sighed. "Even after all this time, I'll still catch a glimpse of her, and it takes me back."

"A glimpse?"

He waved the words away. "Imagination, my wife says. And I suppose she's right. And I'm getting old. Used to be I only thought about her. Or I'd notice someone and see the resemblance. Now I'm starting to see Felicia herself."

Ryan took a step forward without realizing it. "Have you? How often?"

"Oh, no. Just the one time. About a week ago. If it happens again, I'll have to tell my doctor." He picked up the large walking stick and easily held it level. Apparently the man was stronger than he looked.

He was pointing it toward the window across the room. The one which faced the street. "Right there on the sidewalk. Told my wife, too. Made her come look. She said I was imagining things." He sighed. "I probably was. Ahh, who can say? Pass me that book."

It took a second for Ryan to shift gears, but he followed William's sightline to the small table topped by a crossword puzzle dictionary and an illustrated history of China.

"Both of them. Can't do my puzzles if I don't stay sharp."

"No, sir," Ryan said, amused. "This is a wonderful library, by the way. And the house is pretty spiffy, too."

William chuckled. "Spiffy, is it? I agree with you on the library. This room—it's like a treasure to me. The rest of the house? More like an albatross."

Ryan nodded. "I imagine it's difficult to maintain."

William waved a hand. "*Phht.* That's what staff's for. I'd rather move back to Somerset. Grew up there, but my wife loves London. She's determined we keep the place." His shoulders sagged. "Feels like blood money to me. This place should have been Felicia's. That poor girl. Never should have gone down there. You're a good man to have gone after her."

"I tried," Ryan said, feeling the familiar tug of guilt in his stomach. "I failed."

"You tried," William said firmly. "There are a lot who wouldn't even have done that."

"I admired her very much," Ryan admitted. And now he feared that she'd been playing him all along.

He sighed, trying to decide what to say next. He didn't want to tell this kind man that his niece seemed to have resurfaced—and that there was good reason to believe that her sudden reappearance meant that she'd been a spy all those years ago. Not just in intelligence, but actively involved in bringing about the coup.

But did William deserve to know? Would he start imagining her everywhere? That couldn't be good for him.

No, better to stick with his original intent and not tell William anything. Not now. Maybe not ever. Only if it became imperative. Because how the hell could he bear to give such dark news to an old man who'd loved a little girl?

On the other side of the room, the maid rang a bell. "Time for your medicine, Mr. William," she said, going to a sideboard and returning with a glass of water and a tiny paper cup. "Mrs. Carolyn made me promise to remind you to nap. You know what the doctor said."

"The hell I do. I don't even remember the damn appointment."

"I think that's the point, sir." She smiled politely at Ryan. "I'm sorry, but I'm going to have to ask you to cut this short."

"*Hmmph.* My wife's got this one wrapped around her finger. Watches me like a bloody hawk."

"It's fine," Ryan said, making up his mind to stay silent. "Thank you, Mr. Atkinson, for being so hospitable."

"Wait! Wait! Let me write down the number for that estate agent. He can show you the Somerset house. You take a look, now." He scribbled a phone number in the crossword puzzle book, then ripped out the page for Ryan.

"Of course." Ryan folded the note and put it in his pocket. "I'll call right away."

"Good." William beamed. "It was a pleasure to meet you," he added, taking the pills from the maid as Ryan showed himself out.

He waited until he was in the cab to look at the paper, and when he did, he saw a litany of random words filling in the boxes. THECATANDTHEHAT. SUN. ONLY. And on and on and on.

But there *was* a phone number at the top, and that had to mean something. William had made such a point of not only keeping his crossword books, but of keeping them neat. He'd made an exception for Ryan, and the only reason Ryan could deduce was that he was delivering a message.

The number, however, was out of service.

"Fuck."

Maybe it was a safe combination. Maybe it was a code. Maybe it was nonsense from a confused old man. *Double fuck.*

Whatever it was, he'd have to figure it out later.

As the cab pulled up in front of the Stark Century, he folded the paper and shoved it back into his pocket. Then he went inside and settled in at a two-top in the bar. It was still half an hour before noon, and he usually didn't drink at lunch anyway, but today he needed one, and he sipped on a Scotch as Baxter slid into the chair across from him.

"Club soda with lime, thanks," Bax told the waitress. "And a whole slew of ice cubes."

"No problem."

"It still won't be enough ice," he told Ryan as soon as she was out of earshot. "I grew up in Florida. I like a cold drink. And here you go," he added, plunking a cell phone onto the middle of the table without pausing for breath or changing his tone.

"Good work."

"We got lucky. She tossed it in the bin on the corner just one block over. Odd, though."

"What's that?"

"I expected it to be a cheap burner phone, considering the nature of what she was sending you and what we suspect about her. And since I couldn't trace those texts back to anyone. But it seems to be her actual cell phone. Gabriella Anderson's, I mean."

"That is surprising," Ryan said.

"That's not the strangest part." Baxter leaned forward, like a kid sharing a juicy secret about the teacher. "She has a burner app on the phone. That's how she was texting both you and Jamie. One of those apps that lets you have several virtual numbers. And, in the kicker to end all kickers, she didn't pull her SIM card."

"Really?" Ryan leaned back, considering that. He'd told Baxter to find out what he could learn from the phone's card, but he hadn't actually expected they'd get their hands on it. After all, this was a woman who'd been clever enough to fool him as to her role in a coup, then fake her own death and disappear. Why the hell would she leave behind her SIM card?

"What do you think it means?" Baxter asked.

"I wish I knew. Why the hell would a woman who was a spook leave a traceable device for us to find?"

"That's the question of the hour," Baxter agreed. "She had to have known."

"Was there anything unusual embedded in the card?"

Baxter shook his head. "I thought of that—that she was leaving the SIM card on purpose, I mean. But I didn't find anything that could be a message or, well, anything." He swallowed. "There is one other possibility…" He trailed off, leaving Ryan to finish the sentence.

"That she wasn't a spook."

Baxter shrugged. "Could be."

"It could," Ryan agreed. "But I doubt it. To survive that fall? She'd have needed a full-on med-evac team. And the Felicia Cartwright I knew wouldn't have the first clue how to get a fake identity. Not unless they sold it at Harrods."

Baxter considered that, then nodded. "This whole situation's bizarre."

"That it is. Since you mentioned the burner app, I assume you unlocked her phone."

"Hacked her password," Baxter acknowledged. "The phone was mostly stripped. She saw this coming—you said it was her idea to ditch the phone, so she must have been planning it. All photos and files deleted. Her cloud service account deleted. Emails deleted. Just the burner app, the native apps, and a few game apps."

"Gaming? Can we find a handle? We might be able to communicate through one of the apps."

He shook his head. "No, I mean the single-player kind. And not gaming. Games. Well, puzzles, really. Crosswords. Sudoku."

"Crosswords?"

"Yeah. Is that important?"

Ryan thought of William. But how the hell could there be a connection? He shook his head. "Probably not." He sighed. "Well, at least we know one thing for certain."

"What's that?"

"That I have no way to contact her now."

"What's the next step?"

"I'd like you to track down the attorney who handled the probate of Randall's will," Ryan said. "William mentioned that Felicia should have inherited the house, and of course that's true. We should confirm that she would have been the primary beneficiary if she'd survived, and then see if any other Felicias have popped up out of the blue. For that matter, we should see if there's DNA. Randall was wealthy and a little eccentric. Did he freeze sperm? Blood? Brain tissue? Let's find out. This girl says she's Felicia? I want a way to prove it one way or the other."

"Already on the probate question," Baxter said. "I figured you'd ask. Of course, it's Saturday, but I'm making some calls. Hopefully we can get an answer through unofficial channels, because the official ones are locked up tight for the weekend."

"Perfect."

"As for the other, I'll see what I can find out."

"Good man." He swallowed the last of his Scotch, then pushed back his chair.

Baxter cleared his throat, and Ryan hesitated in the act of rising. "Something on your mind?"

"Just, ah, parameters."

"Parameters?" Ryan repeated, hiding his amusement.

"Right. Are we entirely aboveboard on this, sir? Or are you kicking this matter over to Stark Security?"

He knew what Bax was asking. Stark International's security team was very transparent. Very corporate. And very, very aboveboard. Not a lot of Tom Clancyesque maneuvers going down in the hallowed halls of Stark International.

The Stark Security Agency, on the other hand, had been created for a different type of problem. The kind that needed to dig a bit deeper, to cut corners and slice through red tape. The SSA did what was needed to get the job done, and that was okay because the SSA also had a very limited clientele and had the luxury of being extremely selective with its clients.

But still, corners would be cut. And Ryan knew that Baxter had already turned down one offer to join the SSA for exactly that reason. He'd been burned once before, and he was leery of digging himself into another hole so soon after climbing out of one. Ryan respected that. He honored Baxter's request to limit his work to the corporate side of Stark International.

One day, though...

Well, one day, Ryan hoped to convince Baxter to join the SSA. With his particular skills, he'd be a hell of an asset.

As for right now, Ryan just shook his head. "No," he assured his friend. "We're keeping this close and aboveboard. Randall Cartwright's dead. The will's been probated, and that's public record. Harder to get on a weekend, but not impossible or illegal. If it turns out that we have to dig deeper and cross lines, I'll see if Quince can fly over or make a few calls." A former MI6 operative, Quince had been one of the first agents recruited to the SSA. If strings needed to be tugged, he'd know how to do it.

"Sounds good."

"Buzz me when you know something," Ryan added, then headed out while Baxter picked up his own phone to start making more calls.

The mention of Quince, however, stuck in Ryan's brain. As it stood, if Felicia no-showed again, they'd only be able to get in touch if she initiated it.

Unless...

He wondered if Quince could get MI6 to utilize facial recognition software in real time via the traffic cams. It was doubtful they'd be given permission—that would be a hell of a drain on the system—but they could possibly hack in.

He shook his head. He was frustrated and leaping to places he had no business leaping. Not yet. Not until he had a better understanding of what was going on. And why.

Right now, he had to deal with the fact that they were at an impasse. And as he rode up to the penthouse, he consoled himself with the knowledge that he was going to see Jamie, get some lunch, and then head back down at one to, hopefully, meet Felicia.

The Do Not Disturb light was still engaged, and he pressed his keycard to the lock and entered. The place was dead silent, which wasn't surprising considering he'd told Jamie not to move. And Jamie was very good at following directions.

He smiled to himself as he corrected that thought—*when she wanted to be.*

He tossed his jacket on the back of the sofa, ripped off his tie, and started to unbutton his shirt. "Have you been a good girl, Kitten?"

Christ, he was already hard and he wasn't even to the bedroom door yet. Just the anticipation of seeing her like that. Facedown, spread-eagled and wet for him. Knowing that she'd waited. Knowing that she wanted.

He cupped his hand over his cock, now stiff beneath his trousers, then stroked slowly as he crossed to the door. He wanted to open it, then lean against the doorway and tease her with his voice while he took them both almost to the precipice. Then he'd take her from behind, holding her by the waist as he buried himself deep inside her.

"Christ, Kitten," he murmured. "What you do to me."

He paused outside the closed door. "Tell me you want me, Kitten. If you want me to fuck you, I want to hear you say it." He increased the pressure of his hand over his cock, anticipating her words.

Except there were no words.

"Kitten?" He frowned, then called out more loudly, "Jamie. I'm back."

Still nothing. He pushed open the door and saw that she'd turned over onto her back.

But it was the tiny trickle of drool on her stagnant face that had him bursting forward with a terror-filled cry of, "*Jamie!*"

Chapter Thirteen

"Jamie!"

The sharp edge of Ryan's voice pulls me from the thick molasses of sleep in which I'm currently wrapped.

"Jamie, dammit, wake up!"

I shiver, suddenly cold despite the weight of a blanket on me. I'm aware that my back is pressed against the mattress and that is totally against the rules. I try to sit up, jolted into action by the shock of that realization.

Try, yes. But I don't succeed. Instead, it seems as if the blanket is made of lead. I can't seem to make my body do anything. I can't even open my eyes. All I'm aware of is the yellow-gold glow of a light shining down on my still-closed lids.

"Ryan." My mouth is like cotton, and I'm not sure if I've even spoken his name. I try to peel my eyes open, but it's as if they are glued shut. I want to lift my hand so that I can use my fingers to aid my waking, but I can't even manage that.

"Fuck, shit, goddammit." There's panic in his voice—more than I've ever heard—and fear rushes through me, the adrenaline forcing my eyes open.

"Ryan?"

He's standing at the foot of the bed, his eyes on his phone as he sends a text, his expression tense and tight with worry. He doesn't react at all to his name, and that's when I realize I haven't said a single word aloud.

I concentrate, then try again.

"Ryan."

My throat feels like sandpaper and his name comes out low and cracked and broken.

Immediately, he tosses the phone onto the foot of the bed and hurries to my side. "Jamie." He cups my face with his palm, his voice and his expression reflecting both love and terror.

I try to prop myself up, my heart beating faster with a rising panic, but my muscles still aren't working properly. "What's—?"

"You're okay. You're going to be okay."

His words sound like an order rather than a statement, and they do nothing to quell my fear.

He must realize that he's not soothing me, because he draws in a breath. "I'm sorry. I just—when I came in and saw you. And then you didn't wake up even though I kept calling your name and shaking you. Christ, Jamie, can you tell me what happened?"

Now I'm totally confused. "What happened?" My voice is still rough, and he slides off the bed, then hurries to get a bottle of water from the small fridge, ignoring the glass on the table beside the bed. He brings it to me, then helps me sit up enough to swallow.

"I'm okay," I say as he starts to lay me back down. "Just help me scoot back. I don't know what the hell's wrong with me."

His brow furrows as if he's confused, then he sits at the edge of the bed and strokes my hair with one hand as he clutches my fingers with his other. "Kitten, baby, tell me what you remember."

"I did what you said. Facedown on the bed, waiting. I didn't move," I assure him.

A muscle twitches in his cheek. "So you didn't turn over?"

"You made me promise, so I didn't. And then when you spanked me, I thought—" I trail off, managing a pathetic shrug. "I'm sorry I fell asleep. I promise it wasn't you." I offer a small smile. He knows damn well there's nothing about him or his touch that I find sleep inducing.

I expect him to smile in return. Instead, I see a fire in his eyes. And it's not of a passionate nature.

I shift some more, managing to sit up even straighter. "Ryan, what's—?"

But my question is cut off by a loud rap at the door that makes me jump.

"Come in!" Ryan calls.

I hear the snick of the lock and immediately wonder who the hell else has access to our suite. That thought leads to another, but not one I can quite wrap my head around. Just a rising sense of dread. As if there's something bad happening—something horrible and close—and yet I can't quite see it, much less run from it.

"Dustin, thank God. This is my wife, Jamie Hunter. Jamie, this is Dr. Dustin Fields. He's one of the doctors on call for the hotel."

The blanket is already over my breasts—for warmth, not modesty—and I lift it higher. "Um, hi?"

Dr. Fields smiles kindly. I'm guessing that he's a few years older than Ryan, and he has the same confident, competent air about him. He's a man who knows his field—and who's good at his job.

The realization calms me somewhat, pushing away that uncomfortable, enigmatic dread that had been rising inside me.

"Do you mind if I take a look at your eyes, Mrs. Hunter?"

"Jamie," I correct. "And, um, sure."

He gently holds my lid open as he shines a light straight into each eye in turn. It's not unpleasant, but I see spots and blink rapidly when he takes the light away. He asks to see my tongue, and I comply, still uncertain what's going on. He makes a soft noise in his throat that I can't interpret, then pulls out a small leather case.

"I'm going to take a blood sample," he says. "Just in case."

I look at Ryan, my mind racing. "Was I exposed to Ebola or something? Ryan, what's going on?"

Dr. Fields meets Ryan's eyes. "She doesn't know?"

"She's just barely woken up."

The doctor nods, then starts to stand. Ryan stops him. "No. Please. Take your sample. And tell me what you think."

"I think it was simply a sleeping agent. A strong one, but she's showing no signs of poison and seems to be recovering quickly."

He's right. I'm feeling more alert by the second. Even so, his words don't make sense, and as he takes my arm to draw a blood sample, I tell him so. "I didn't eat or drink anything that would make me sleep."

Ryan and the doctor exchange another look.

"Dammit, Ryan. What is going on?"

"I wasn't in the room with you, Jamie."

Fear spikes through me, and I start to shake. "What are you talking about?" I pull the blanket up, hugging it to me, but it's not enough, and Ryan moves closer to sit with his back against the headboard as well. He pulls me close, and I snuggle against him, and it's only then—in my husband's arms—that I finally manage to get my trembling under control.

He still hasn't answered me, and when I feel strong enough to handle whatever he says, I lift my head. "You still haven't told me. What happened?"

He sighs, as if this is the last thing he wants to talk about, but then he nods. More to himself than to me. As if he's mentally ordering himself to do something he doesn't want to do at all. Then he turns a bit so that he can press my hand to his chest. "It's my fault."

"What? How?"

"That bitch—Gabby. Felicia. Whoever the fuck she is. I talked to her."

I shake my head, confused. But whether from the drug or his words, I'm not sure.

"Earlier, right after I left, I tried one more time to text her. That time, she answered. She said she wanted to meet right then. I told her I wasn't there, and we agreed to meet at one. Downstairs in the bar."

I look over at the clock. It's ten past twelve.

I must look blank because Ryan explains. "She knew I was out. Most likely she was watching the hotel and already knew that, but I confirmed it in our text conversation." There's pure steel in his voice. "She got in here and she drugged you. Jamie, you were out cold. I knew something was wrong when you didn't answer when I called. And then I saw your face…"

He shivers. "I swear to God, I'm going to find that bitch and I'm going to make her pay."

"Hunter, no. Nothing you've said proves it was Gabby."

"Kitten, baby, you're not thinking straight." The steel is gone, replaced by such sweet tenderness it makes me want to weep.

I draw an unsteady breath, then shake my head. "I shouldn't be thinking straight, you're right. I've been violated and exposed, touched and manipulated." I hug myself, the voicing of these words making them all too real.

"I could have been raped, Ryan. Hell, I could have been killed." I pause, then take long, choking gulps of air. Everything I've just said is true, and that knowledge burns through me, making me want to both kick and scream and bash down walls even while I want to curl up into a ball, hide, and never come out again. But I can't—*I just can't*—believe what he's suggesting. "Do you think I'd be arguing with you if I thought for a second it could be her?"

I drank beer by the pool with Gabby. I house-sat her cat. She had our spare key for an entire semester. She lent me money when I was short and showed me how to change my wiper blades. That is not a woman who could violate a friend like that. It's just not Gabby.

"You're wrong," I tell him again. "It can't be Gabby. She wouldn't do this. Not to me. Not to anyone."

"It's been a long time since you knew her," he says, his voice pitched as the voice of reason. "And all things considered, she's a hell of an actress."

"No," I say, determined not to believe it. Not out of stubbornness but because it just can't *be.* "And how would she have gotten in, anyway?"

"Who knows how long she was planning this? That door was accessed with a cloned maid's key—and damned if I'm not going to figure out how that could happen. Plus the door wasn't bolted from the inside." He actually smiles a little bit at that. "Unless you broke the rules and got up."

My cheeks flame as I glance up at Dr. Fields, certain that he totally understands the subtext of this particular conversation. "I didn't cheat," I say primly.

"I know." Ryan draws a breath, and I can see the anger flowing through him. A wild, restrained anger at himself for what he holds as his fault. The kind of fury he can hold in for a while, but eventually, it's going to erupt. "It was her," he continues, "and I pretty much announced that you were alone, then gave her an open invitation to walk in here, inject you with something, and walk right back out again."

"No."

"*Yes,*" he says, and I hear the anger in his voice. "Jamie, listen to me. I called her Felicia in the conversation. And she didn't correct me."

"No. No, that doesn't make any sense. None of this does."

"There's more proof," he says, making my insides twist. "We got her cell phone. She ditched it, but we were able to track the location."

I shake my head. "So?"

"So we got past her security. The phone had its main number and virtual numbers. She was texting us both from the same phone. Baxter scrolled through after he cracked it. The original text to get me to meet her. The text with you about the cafe. Another to me in the car. Different numbers. One phone."

I want to cry. "I don't understand. Whether she's Gabby or Felicia, why drug me? It made me sick, sure, but if you'd been gone all day, eventually I would have just woken up on my own. Right?" I look to the doctor for confirmation, and he nods. "Then what was the point?"

"A warning," he says. "But I'll be damned if I can figure out her endgame."

Chapter Fourteen

None of this makes sense, which is what I tell Ryan when he returns to the bedroom after seeing Dr. Fields out.

"Doesn't it?" His tone is harsh. As sharp as a blade. He's terrified for me and angry at himself. And all of that is coming right back out. "If I'm right and she was a spy aligned with the dissidents who killed Mikal, then she knows how the system works."

"What the hell does that mean?"

"I mean that she understands that I can get my hands on the resources to help her. To get whatever she needs to help her disappear again. But she has to know that's not something I'm terribly motivated to do after being double-crossed all those years ago. Maybe she thinks I need an incentive. Maybe she knows that I would do anything to keep you safe. Any. Fucking. Thing. And maybe she'd be right."

I swallow, because of course I know that's true. And knowing it makes me feel safe despite all of this.

"So my friend Gabby used to be Felicia." I don't like saying it, but considering the phone thing, I guess it's true. "But why study history? Why work as a professor now?"

"Academia's a good place to hide. And if she's still active in intelligence, it's a good cover job. And in the States? That's a lot of space to hide if you need to, no passport required."

I hug my knees to my chest. Every one of his arguments makes sense, but all I can do is shake my head. "I don't want to believe it."

He sighs. "I know, Kitten." He goes to the bedroom's coffee station and brews me a cup. He brings it over, then sits on the edge of the bed facing me as I sip it slowly. I don't taste it at all, but I appreciate the way it seems to chase off the cold that still flows through me.

Dr. Fields says that's a remnant of the sedative, but I know he's wrong. It's fear, and it's running through my veins like water. Someone got into our room. Someone got into my body.

Another violent tremble rips through me and I slosh coffee onto the crisp, white hotel sheets, then snap out a curse. Because that's how it is now. One second, I'm calm—or angry. The next, I'm wracked with fear.

"It's okay." His voice is warm and soothing as he gently takes the cup. He sets it aside, then eases up next to me, his arm around my shoulder.

"It's not okay," I argue. "Nothing's okay right now."

He puts a finger under my chin, then moves my head until I'm looking him in the eyes. "We are," he says, and the certainty in his voice takes my breath away.

I nod, because yes. *Yes.* Despite everything, we're fine. And together we'll get through this.

I'm just not sure how.

"Let's go to the living room," Ryan says now. "I'll call housekeeping to bring fresh sheets."

"It's okay. It's just a splash."

He shifts on the bed, then cups my face, looking hard into my eyes. "I'm so, so sorry."

"It's not your fault."

"Isn't it? Christ, Jamie, I don't know."

"What do you mean? Because you casually said you weren't in the hotel room? That doesn't make what happened your fault."

"I'm not sure about that," he says. "But it wasn't what I was thinking about."

"Then what?"

He shakes his head, his hands in front of him as if he's trying to capture the bubble of an idea but can't quite make it happen.

He sighs as he slips off the bed, then drags his fingers through his short, dark hair. He stands at the foot of the bed, his expression more miserable than I've ever seen it.

"Hunter? You're scaring me. And considering I was already scared, that's saying a lot."

His lips twitch, and he nods. "I should never have let you stay. I knew—goddammit, I knew—that this situation with Felicia could go south fast. But I saw you standing in that damn bar, your voice in my ear and sex on your mind, and—well, Kitten, you know damn well it wasn't reason on my mind then. It was you. Only you."

"I still don't understand."

"I know." He sighs. "The problem is, neither do I. But when a woman pops back into your life after more than a decade demanding your help—"

I try to think about his words—to forget about the Gabby I know and think about what he's saying. "You think she's unstable? That you should have expected she'd hurt me because I've taken her place, and that doesn't fit the fiction in her mind?"

"No. Not, not exactly." He takes a breath, and I think he's going to continue. Instead, he says, "I need a drink. And I don't even know if I can offer you one because—"

He cuts himself off with a disgusted expression.

"Hunter…" I move to the foot of the bed and reach for him. I'm naked, and I watch as his eyes skim over me, his expression an odd mix of sadness and arousal.

"You're mine, dammit. Aren't you mine?"

"Yes. Always. You know that."

His fingers trail up my body—from my hip, following the curve of my waist, then up higher to cup my breast.

I draw in a shaky breath, growing passion quelling my lingering fear as my body comes alive with need. He brushes his thumb over my nipple, then bends over and presses the softest, sweetest kiss against my lips.

"Mine," he repeats. "And I take care of what's mine."

I close my eyes as understanding washes over me. As I see deep into the heart of what he fears. "I'm fine." I take his hand from my breast and lift it, then kiss his palm. "I'm right here, and I'm safe. All she did was make me sleep."

He lifts his head until his eyes meet mine, firm and hard. "But it could have been a hell of a lot worse."

"You couldn't know that."

"Dammit, Jamie, that's my point." He closes his eyes, presses his fingers to his temple, then turns and marches into the living room. He pours a shot of whiskey, then slams it back. I hurry into the hotel robe and follow him, reaching his side right as he's poured another.

"Me, too?"

"Sure, why not? Then I can fail you on that count, too, when Dr. Fields calls and tells me he's checked the labs, and I need to keep you away from alcohol for a while."

I look at him, and the misery on his face breaks my heart. "Oh, Hunter." I ease up behind him and slide my arms around his waist. "You didn't fail me. I know you love me. I know you'll always protect me."

"I would die for you," he whispers, and I feel tears well in my eyes.

"I know that, too," I say, a lump rising in my throat. "But don't you dare."

He spins in my arms to face me, and one hand holds me around my neck as the other tugs open my robe. I draw in breath, my body warm with anticipation. He pushes the sides of the robe open, intentionally grazing the swell of my breasts with each motion. Then he slowly—so wonderfully, horribly slowly—eases a fingertip lower and lower, tracing a lazy path until he reaches my waxed mons.

I bite my lower lip, anticipating a further journey south, only to jump when his phone chimes with an incoming text.

"Damn." His low curse is barely audible, but it echoes my sentiments so exactly that I feel my core clench in response to the heat in his voice.

He pulls out his phone as I decide to finish what he started, rolling my hips as I press my fingertip where his was only moments before, then ease lower and lower, until I can slide my finger over my own slick folds.

"Naughty," he says as he puts his phone away, then tugs my hand away to lead me toward the sofa as I whimper in protest.

"Was that Baxter?" I know that Hunter's asked Baxter to look at the elevator video surveillance to locate Gabby before or after she attacked me. Since I'm still hoping that she didn't, I'm hoping she won't be there.

"It was Dr. Fields. He was right. Just a sedative, and one that's quickly metabolized."

"Thank God," I say. "Pour me a drink."

He laughs, and though I expect him to tell me to wait another day, he returns to the bar and complies. I guess under the circumstances, he figures I need it.

While he pours, I sit, cinching the robe as I do. As much as I want Hunter's hands on me, right now, I want to know what's going on even more.

"Have you thought about how to prove that Gabby's Felicia? If she doesn't admit it, I mean."

"I'm hoping some of Randall's DNA turns up," he says. "If he stored any biological matter, it should be easy to test."

"And if he didn't?"

"Still possible. Felicia had a birthmark."

I raise my brows. "Did she?" I can't keep the amusement out of my voice. "So, where was this birthmark?"

"Jamie."

"No, really. I'm very interested."

"Her breast," he says flatly.

"Ah." I open the robe again, exposing my own breast. "Like here?" I brush the swell of my breast, which would easily be exposed in a simple scoop-neck T-shirt.

"No."

"Here?" I slide my finger a few inches toward my nipple. Any dress that would reveal a mark there would definitely be considered daring.

"Jamie…"

"Or maybe here." I trace my finger over my areola and watch as Ryan swallows. "Interesting place for a birthmark," I say. "Kind of her to show you for confirmation."

"Jamie, please." He sets my drink on the table. "You know I—"

I burst out laughing, then take his hands and tug him down onto the couch beside me. Then I straddle him, my robe still open. I take his hand and close it over my breast, then draw in a sharp breath from his touch.

"I love you," he says, taking his hand from my breast and replacing it with his mouth. I arch back, holding his shoulder with one hand as I use the other to tug on the robe's sash and pull it all the way open. I'm naked beneath it, and as I slide forward, I feel the hard length of his cock straining against his slacks. I squirm, wanting to feel him—to feel us. Wanting to erase all of this craziness even if just for a moment.

Mostly, I want to feel Hunter inside me. I want him to claim me. want to feel safe.

The last thought comes unbidden, and while it's true, it also sparks a new flurry of questions. And though I want to push them aside in favor of the rising heat and my wild, demanding need, the question trips from my lips. "I still don't get why she'd resurface," I say as Hunter moves to kiss me.

His mouth closes hard over mine. "I… have… a few thoughts… on that," he says, his words coming out breathy between his assault on my ips. He breaks the kiss long enough to look at me and say, "But can you please wait to hear them until after I fuck you?"

I nod, giddy, and he grabs my ass with one hand and supports my back with his other as he rises from the couch. I wrap my legs around him, and he carries me to the bedroom, then drops me, laughing, onto the bed. He wastes no time stripping, then climbs on top of me.

"Kitten," he murmurs, only to curse when his work phone chimes. "Put it on speaker," I say. Because we both know it's either about Felicia—or it is her.

He's breathing hard when he connects the call and says, "Hunter. What have you got for me?"

"It's Baxter. I've been reviewing the footage on your floor surrounding the time of Jamie's attack, and we found the incident. We have footage of the intruder manipulating the lock and entering."

"And?"

"The intruder wasn't a woman, sir. It's most definitely a man."

Chapter Fifteen

Hunter orders Baxter up to the suite, then ends the call. For a moment he says nothing. Then he leaves the bedroom. I hesitate, wanting to follow but unsure what he needs right then. But then I tell myself, *Fuck it.* Because no matter what else, I know he needs me.

I find him standing in front of the closed balcony door, looking out at the London skyline. I ease up behind him and put my arms around his waist. For a moment, he simply stands there. Then he puts his hands over mine.

"It wasn't Gabby," I say.

"Maybe not. Or maybe it was, and she—*Felicia*—sent a man to the room."

"Dammit, Ryan." I release him, then move to his side, my body angled so that I can see both his face and his reflection in the glass. "I believe you, okay. She was Felicia, she went under, she came back up as Gabby." I don't like it, but I can't logically argue it. Not after the phone thing. "But maybe there's more to it than that."

"Like what?"

I shrug, then move to the sitting area and park myself on the edge of the coffee table. "Maybe she wasn't in intelligence. Maybe she just somehow, survived. Maybe she had amnesia and only recently got her memory back. Maybe the dissidents were tracking her down. I don't know. But maybe she's not some stone-cold spy. Maybe she's simply a girl who tried to carve out a new life."

"Jamie…" He trails off, shaking his head as he walks toward me.

"No, don't patronize me. I could be right. I mean, it's a real possibility, isn't it?"

"It's a possibility. I don't know how real."

I take a deep breath, happy to have earned even that small concession. "I know you don't believe me, but I'm certain Gabby wouldn't hurt me. And now we know that she didn't."

"Not directly, but that doesn't mean she didn't pull the strings."

"No." I shake my head. "*No.*" Anger is firing in me again, but I'm not sure if it's at him or at whoever drugged me. I don't care. Honestly, it feels good to let it out. "I *know* her. And now you're shoving her into this Felicia mold that you've constructed. You've built this Spy Felicia persona up, and you're painting Gabby to be evil just so you can erase some of your goddamn guilt. Because if she manipulated it all back then, it means that none of it was your fault."

He flinches and I recoil, unable to believe I actually said that.

"Ryan, I—"

But I don't know how to finish the sentence. It doesn't matter anyway, because he's gone pasty white, and I watch as he turns from me, then goes into the bedroom.

Shit.

I wait a moment, debating, then go after him. He's sitting on the edge of the bed, his head down, his forehead resting on his fingertips.

"Hunter." His name is soft, barely audible, but he looks up, and there's no expression on his face. His eyes, however, are full of pain, and I wish I could call the words back. Could make it all better.

He draws a deep breath, then holds out a hand for me. I hate myself right now, but I take it hesitantly, and he pulls me to him, across the wide rift that has opened up between us and into his arms.

"I'm sorry," I whisper. "I didn't mean that. I'm frustrated and scared and—"

"*No.* You're right. For so long I've thought that I failed her. All the trust she put into me, and I couldn't save her. But if it was an extraction, I didn't fail her. She manipulated me, but I didn't fail her."

"No," I say. "You didn't."

"But none of that matters now. Honestly, it would have been better if I'd shot her in the face myself all those years ago."

I frown, confused by both his words and the knife edge in his voice. "I don't follow."

"I told you when this all started that you should leave. That at some point, she'd try to use you for leverage. Remember?"

I nod. I'd refused to go.

"Well, she's only here now because I didn't see what she truly was. I didn't stop her years ago when I had the chance. And now she's come back—or she's sent some flunky—to show me just how easy it is to get to you."

"You told me earlier that you didn't know her endgame."

"I'm beginning to figure it out," he says, looking not at me but some point beyond, as if he's seeing a movie of the answers playing out in front of him.

"This whole thing started less than a week ago when she contacted me wanting help. Either things have changed, or this is her way of saying that I don't have any choice but to help." His eyes go hard. "The plan didn't work. All it did was make me dangerous."

I pull him up off the bed, then hook my arms around his waist as I look into those icy blue eyes. "You weren't dangerous before?"

He meets my gaze, his smile thin. "Oh, I was. And if Felicia remembers our time together, she damn well knows it."

A tremble cuts through me, and I clutch him tighter, then rest my head against his chest. "That's the hard part, isn't it? That you liked her? I mean, she was more than just a job. And that makes it all worse."

My eyes are closed, but I can feel him nod. "I did. She was sharp, easy to talk to. And I believed she was an innocent trapped in one version of hell. God, when she went into that river..."

He trails off, the pain in his voice still lingering in the air.

"I'm sorry," I say, meaning it, even though I know it doesn't help.

He brushes a kiss over the top of my head, then sighs. "I thought I had a better sense of people, but it never once occurred to me that she might be playing me. Using me for an extraction—hell, using me at all."

I look up to see his frown deepen.

"I may have screwed up before and not seen the truth, but that was a long time ago. And whatever the fuck's going on now, she's damn well not dragging my wife into the middle of it."

"Except I'm already in the middle. I know Gabby." I frown. "Let's say Gabby's innocent—I know you don't believe that but go with me for a second."

He nods.

"If Felicia's coming into the cold—"

"In *from the cold*," he corrects. "How can you not know that? The book? The movie?"

I make a whooshing motion over my head.

"John le Carré. *The Spy Who Came in from the Cold.* You've seen every movie ever made."

"I missed one or two, I think. My point is that if she's out in the world, she needs an identity, right? Maybe she latched on to Gabby because they do look so much alike. Maybe she ran across her picture somewhere and thought, oh, yeah, I can be that girl. Maybe your Felicia is the one Gabby's scared of."

"*That* sounds like the plot to a movie," he says, making me laugh. "And you're forgetting that the Gabby texts to you and the Felicia texts to me originated on the same phone."

"Well, hell." I drag my fingers through my hair as I think, but I don't have any answers.

I take this opportunity to pull on some ratty PJs. Comfort clothes, because this has been one hell of a day, and even with Hunter watching my back, I still feel vulnerable. Then I pull the robe on over all that. Just one more barrier against a world in which even Ryan can't always protect me.

"Should we call the cops? Or whatever they're called in London?"

Ryan shakes his head. "Not yet. Not until I understand exactly what's going on. If there's espionage at the heart of this, I want to be able to maneuver. I don't want to be constrained at all if your safety is on the line."

I nod, understanding what he means. Get the police involved, and there are rules. Get Stark Security up and running and things can happen in the shadows.

"I understand," I say. "And I have another question. Well, an idea, actually. What if Felicia wasn't supposed to have come in from the cold— see? I remembered that time. And someone wants her to disappear again?"

He nods. "I've thought about that. Felicia is a spy. She resurfaces. But someone isn't happy about that. They want her dead. So they attack you, hoping that we'd believe Felicia was behind it. Make me angry enough and maybe I'll do part of their work for them. Finish off what I thought the river already accomplished."

"Right. They think you'll kill her," I say, my mind going over every Hollywood thriller movie I've watched and script I've read. "That they can trick you into making that happen."

"It's a theory," Ryan says. "Convoluted, maybe, but I've heard a lot of strange theories in my day, and more often than I expected, they turned out to be true."

I hug myself. "But if they wanted to piss you off enough that you'd go all Liam Neeson on her, they would have actually killed me." A shiver wracks my body. "Ryan, all of this—"

There's a rap on the door, and he takes my hands. "I know, Kitten. But we're going to get through this. Okay?"

"I know we will," I say, because I do. Because even though everything is fucked up and weird, I trust Hunter. Always.

"Come on," he says, leading me into the living room. "Let's see what Baxter has to say."

I sit on the sofa with Ryan while Baxter settles into an armchair across from us. He's in his late twenties, with the kind of face that seems forgettable until you've seen it a couple of times. Unlike Ryan, whose hard lines and angles give him a commanding, powerful appearance, Baxter's face is more like the guy next door. But his eyes are sharp and intelligent, his mouth wide and sensual. And every once in a while, he flashes a dimple that makes me certain he was the kind of kid who could get away with anything back in school.

I don't know his background, but I know that Ryan is actively recruiting him for Stark Security, even though Baxter says he's content on the corporate security side. But he must be good because my husband is not one to extend an offer for Stark Security to slouches.

That means Baxter's had training, but whether it was private or military, I don't know. What I am certain of is that he has skills, and I'm grateful that he's part of the team.

"Well?" I say, prompting Baxter. "How do you know my attacker was a man?"

"We know the approximate time of the attack based on Ryan's movements and what Dr. Fields told us about the metabolism of the drug. So it was relatively simple to review the hotel's security footage. And the best part is that we got a face. He looked straight at one of the hidden cameras."

I look between the two men. "But that's incredible. I mean, wouldn't someone coming to do something like that to me assume we'd check the security cameras? You'd think he'd keep his head down, right?"

"He did," Baxter says. "Hat on in the elevator, head down. We never saw his face. From the time he went through the lobby until he got close to your door. But that's when he looked up—just once—and one of the hall cameras got a sweet shot."

"Do you know who he is?" I ask.

Ryan looks to Baxter, who shakes his head. "Not yet. But I sent the image to the SSA," he adds, referring to the Stark Security Agency.

He passes me his phone. The guy's standing far enough away that he's not too distorted from the fisheye lens, but I don't recognize him. It's a black and white photo, but his hair is light enough that I assume it's blond. He has thick eyebrows and a round face with a pointed chin. He's not particularly attractive, but neither is he unattractive. Basically, he's the kind of guy you'd never notice. I certainly never have and say as much.

"Denny's running it through facial recognition," Baxter tells me, referring to one of Stark Security's agents in LA. "Hopefully, she'll get a hit soon."

"Hopefully," I repeat, then lean in as Ryan puts his arm around me. "What do we do until then?" I frown, remembering. "Didn't you set a meeting with Felicia? Or Gabby? Or—well, do you think she'll keep it?"

"I thought she might. If only to make her seem less complicit in drugging you. But she's not here yet."

"Are you sure?"

He nods. "I've got hotel security keeping an eye open. No sign of her yet."

"Oh. I guess that makes her look more guilty, huh?"

He doesn't answer, and I sigh. His silence is answer enough.

"So how do you find her now?"

"Without a contact number, all we can do is wait."

"I have a bit of additional news," Baxter says as I sigh with frustration. "I tracked down the probate attorney and the executor of Randall's will. Name's Marjorie Smythe."

"That was fast."

"Haven't heard back, but I asked her to call me as soon as she could. Told her it was urgent."

"Fingers crossed," I say, then jump when the chime of the suite's doorbell fills the room.

Ryan stands, then hurries toward the door.

I run into the bedroom to change into jeans and a T-shirt and am only half-dressed when I hear the door slam. I jump a mile, then yank on my T-shirt without a bra and race back into the main room as a woman screams. Or, rather, she starts to scream. It's cut off at the same time as I hear a body slam against a wall.

I reach the front hall at the same time as Baxter. Bax continues, but I freeze at the sight in front of me—Ryan pressed against Gabby—Felicia?— his arm hard over her neck, his face contorted into fury.

"This is the end, Felicia," he demands, his voice hard. "It's time for you to tell us what the fuck is going on."

Chapter Sixteen

"Goddammit," Hunter growls, his huge hand cupping Gabby's throat as he presses her against the now-closed door, as one of the hotel's security guards stands at attention a few feet away.

I make a yelping noise, and Baxter—who's beside me—takes a step forward. But Hunter shifts his gaze from the woman long enough to shoot us both a quelling look. I freeze, and Baxter, who's no slouch, stops moving, too. We both know that right now, my husband is as dangerous as he's ever been.

Slowly, he turns to the guard. "You found her where?"

"In the lobby, sir."

He shifts back to face Gabby, his expression as hard as steel. "You think you can threaten me? Attack my wife?" Hunter continues, his voice so low and dangerous that goose bumps pop on my skin. "Do you truly believe that you can pull that kind of bullshit and there won't be any consequences? It may have been more than a decade, Felicia, but I would have thought your memory was better. I would have thought you'd know exactly what I'll do to protect what's mine."

His grip isn't tight enough to prevent her from swallowing, and I watch as her throat moves and tears flood her eyes.

"Ryan," Baxter says softly. "Let her talk."

Ryan glances sideways at Baxter, his face still lined with fury. Then he shifts his gaze, and his eyes soften as he meets mine. A moment passes, and he turns back to Gabby. "You want to talk? Fine. But I don't want to hear any more bullshit about how you need my help. Fuck that. We're done. I want answers and I want them now, or I swear to God I'll break your fucking neck."

I believe him. Hunter's not the kind of man who would hurt a woman, but this is different. This time, I'm the one he's protecting, and know damn well that he'll do whatever is necessary to keep me safe. Tha she's a woman—maybe even my friend—isn't even an issue. More that that, if he truly believes that the only way to ensure I'm safe is to kill her he'll do that, too, without even hesitating.

Right now, though, I fear he might hurt her out of pure fury, because I can see his temper rising as she stays silent. The realization both scare and humbles me. As a rule, Hunter's one of the most in-control men I'v ever known. But he's on a precipice, about to spin out of control, and know that it's mostly about me.

"Hunter," I whisper. "She can't answer."

It takes a moment, but my words penetrate, and he loosens th pressure on her neck. "Talk," he says.

Her shoulders relax slightly as she draws in a breath, then nods.

"Why the fuck are you here, Felicia?"

She licks her lips. "We were going to meet in the bar." She look toward me, her expression terrified. "All I did was come to meet you a the bar. We were supposed to talk."

"About what exactly? How you hired someone to drug my wife?"

She shakes her head, looking a lot like a terrified rabbit.

"It's okay, Gabby," I say gently. "Whatever it is just say it."

She flashes a tiny smile my way, her eyes full of gratitude. "That' exactly it," she says. "I *am* Gabriella Anderson. Not Felicia. I swear on m father's memory—*both* my fathers—that I'm not Felicia Cartwright."

* * * *

For a moment, no one says a word.

Then I see Ryan's face tighten and his arm move. I hurry forward an grab him before he can pin her to the wall again. "No," I say. "Let he talk. Gabby, go sit over there."

I nod toward the seating area, and she hurries that direction, shootin me a grateful smile.

"I'm okay," Ryan says, tugging his arm free. I study him, wary, bu ultimately step back, realizing he's wrangled himself in, his fury shiftin into a tentative calm.

"Listen first," I say. "Then questions. Promise?"

"No," he says, then walks toward her, leaving me to trail behind while Baxter dismisses the guard.

He takes a seat in the chair opposite the sofa while I sit next to Gabby. I'm probably stupid to trust her, but I do. I really do. And right now, she just looks miserable. And scared.

"I'm listening," Ryan says in a slow voice that edges up on dangerous.

"I'm not Felicia," she repeats. "My name is Gabriella Anderson. I'm her twin."

I see my own confusion reflected in Baxter's face. And I expect to see the same on Ryan's. Instead, his expression is carefully blank. "Try again," he says. "Felicia was an only child."

"No, but she thought she was. I thought I was an only child, too." Her voice is steady and she's looking straight into his eyes. "And if you'll stop interrupting me, I'll tell you what I know."

His eyes widen. I'm probably the only one who would notice, but I can tell he's impressed with the way she's handling herself. He says nothing for a moment then asks, "Is she really dead?"

"Yes. Or, at least, I assume so. My father told me she was. Well, actually, what he told me was that if my sister wasn't dead, it was because you faked her death. I'm guessing you didn't fake it?"

Ryan shakes his head. "No." That simple word holds a world of regret.

Gabby draws a breath, nodding as she looks at him, her expression compassionate. "I figured," she whispers. "But I hoped that maybe..." She shakes her head as if clearing cobwebs. "Anyway, Daddy told me about what you did for her. I guess Randall told him all about it. And my father said that if anyone tried to—well, if they tried to hurt me, that you'd help me."

"Why would people be trying to hurt you?"

She swallows. "I don't know."

"How do you know I'm not one of those people?"

"I—I wasn't sure at first," she says. "But now...honestly, if you were going to kill me, I guess I'm banking that I'd already be dead."

"*Hmm.*" A muscle twitches in Hunter's cheek, and I can practically see all the questions in his mind: if she's truly not Felicia, why didn't she mention that when they first met? Why did she send a text signed *F*? Why did she answer to that name in their recent text conversation? And why doesn't she know why she's in danger?

That's not what he asks, though. Instead, he says, "Why did you think you were an only child?"

Baxter stands before she can speak. "Not that I want to miss this story, but I should probably go check on the progress of that computer search we're doing."

It takes me a second to remember that they're running a facial recognition check on the man who injected me. When I do, I flash Baxter a smile of gratitude, hoping he understands, as I don't want to say anything about that part of this convoluted story with Gabby in the room. Just in case she's not as innocent as I hope she is.

"Good plan," Ryan says. "Let me know as soon as you have something solid."

Baxter nods, and the moment he's out of the room, Ryan's attention turns back to Gabby. "You say you're Felicia's twin, yet you thought you were an only child," he presses. "Explain that one. Or, actually, just start at the beginning."

"I am. I will. I mean, it's all twisted up. But the thing is, I didn't even know about Felicia until a few weeks ago. Felicia's dad—Randall Cartwright—was married to my mother. Her name's Allison. And I guess she had an affair with Randall's best friend, Jeff Anderson."

"And Jeff's your father?"

She nods.

"And Allison got pregnant," I add.

"Exactly. With twins." She draws a deep breath. "The thing is, Randall is worth a fortune, and he was also super private. He was furious with my dad—this is all stuff my dad told me, I never met Randall—and cut ties with him. But my mother—our mother—died after having us. And the thing is, they didn't know which man actually fathered the babies. So they split us up. I went with Jeff to the States, and Felicia stayed with Randall in London."

"Why didn't they run a paternity test?"

"I asked my dad that before he—well, before. And he said that Randall didn't want to know. I think he was afraid that we weren't his. Or that Felicia wasn't. I mean, he pretty much gave up on me."

"And you didn't know any of this growing up?" Ryan asks.

She shakes her head. "I've only known for a few weeks. My dad—I mean, Jeff—he and I were driving about a month ago. He'd been edgy and out of sorts. He said we both needed a vacation and he'd reserved us a cabin. I'm on a sabbatical and he said it would be a great chance to dig in and organize my research for a book I'm writing. A treatise on some important manuscripts that—never mind. The point is we were going to stay there for a couple of months."

"Months?"

She nods. "But it never happened. We—well, we ended up in a horrible accident and didn't make it. We were run off the road by some crazy person driving like a maniac."

"Drunk driver?" I ask.

"I thought so, but later Dad said it was intentional. I don't know. I only—"

"Take a breath," Ryan says gently. "And tell us what happened, step by step."

"Right. Okay. Well, I got thrown clear. Just bruises and a sprained wrist. I mean, I was exceptionally lucky. But my dad..." She trails off to wipe tears from her eyes. "He was bad off. Really bad. He didn't even make it to the hospital. He told me—"

Her breath hitches as a sob wracks her body. "He told me that he loved me, but that he wasn't my father. He told me the whole story, then added that he'd stayed in touch with some of Randall's staff all these years. He wanted to keep an eye on Felicia. After all, back then for all he knew, she was his, too."

"So he'd heard about her death."

She nods. "Plus it made the papers. But there weren't any details. Not about you, I mean," she added, nodding to Ryan. "Anyway, her death shook him, and he had a paternity test done—I thought we were just doing it for one of those genealogical websites. And it turned out that our father was Randall. But he didn't tell me any of that at the time. Could I have some water?"

"Sure." I get up to get it while she continues.

"He got in touch with Randall and told him. I guess he thought it might soothe Randall's grief to know I was out there. But Randall never contacted me. And Daddy said they never talked again. But before the ambulance got there, he told me I was in danger."

"Danger, how?"

She shakes her head. "He didn't say. You have to understand that I'm cleaning this conversation up. He was in pain. In and out of consciousness. He was talking, but a lot of it was nonsense. I think the only thing keeping him going was worry about me. It was hard to figure what he was saying. And I was scared and woozy, too. But a couple of things stood out. He said that Randall had a private attorney. A friend. And that I needed to talk to him. He said it was vital. He even used that word."

"What's his name?"

"He never said."

I return with the water, then sit on the arm of Ryan's chair.

She takes a sip before continuing. "I asked over and over, but...well, I don't think he could remember. He only said I had to talk to the lawyer. And that I had to be careful. And he said that I should find you," she adds to Ryan. "That you'd do for me what you did for Felicia. And then...and then he was gone."

A single tear tracks down her cheek, and she closes her eyes before continuing. "I had no idea how to find you, so I started with Google. And it wasn't hard. You were there. And the really wild thing was that I learned you two were married," she adds, with a nod to me. "I found Nikki's number and called her and said I wanted to surprise you. And I asked for Ryan's work number so I could set up this fake surprise through him."

"Why not call me?" I ask.

"It was such a weird coincidence that I guess I felt awkward. It's been a lot of years. Plus, I'd seen online that Ryan was in London, and I was here, too. I'd come over after the accident because I figured whoever had run us off the road wouldn't expect me to hide all the way across the ocean."

She downs the rest of her water. "Also, I wanted to see where I was born."

"You went to Randall's townhouse," Ryan says, and it's not a question. "Did you talk to your uncle?"

"I wanted to. I thought about it. But I chickened out."

I nod in understanding, then try to get us back on thread. "So you got Ryan's work number from Nikki and sent a text, right?"

"Right. I'd gotten spooked. I was sure someone was following me, and when there was a break-in at the B&B I was staying at, I completely freaked out. I switched to a cheap hotel, and that's when I got up the nerve to text Ryan." She shrugs. "I only knew that it was a work line. I didn't know if a text would even go through. But I tried that first because

I was too scared to actually call."

She looks between me and Ryan. "But you answered, and I was incredibly relieved. And we were going to meet at that pub."

"In the text, you told me that I'd helped you before. Why?"

"I didn't think you'd show for a stranger. And if you thought I was Felicia when you first saw me, I figured you'd at least stay."

"But you never showed."

She swallows. "I chickened out."

"Why?" I ask.

"Because of what Daddy said. About how you'd do the same for me as you did for Felicia. I—he'd told me the story about how you went down there and married her and tried to save her. But he was messed up. He was really bad. There was so much blood…"

We both give her a moment to collect herself, then I gently say, "Go on."

"I was afraid. His last words were *find the lawyer, find Felicia's husband, be careful.* And I was confused because before he'd said you'd helped her. Maybe I'd misunderstood and he was trying to warn me away. Because what if you'd hurt Felicia? What if *you* were the one who wanted to hurt me?"

"That's why you didn't show," Ryan says.

"I left a note." She shrugs. "Later, I called Nikki back and that's when I learned that Jamie was coming in. And I figured I could get with Jamie and get a sense of you. Of whether you'd help me."

"Except you're forgetting about how you tried to get me back to the pub. The same day you met Jamie. Why did you pull another no-show? And why did you sign that text with an F for Felicia?"

Gabby's brow furrows. "But—what? I didn't."

"Do *not* fuck with me," Ryan says, then pulls out his phone. He swipes to the text I saw—the one that sent me over the edge—and he shoves the phone at her.

Her eyes widen as she reads, then she looks between both of us, hunching in on herself so that she seems like a terrified rabbit. "I didn't send that," she says. "I swear." She grapples for the small backpack she probably uses as a purse. "Here. You can look for yourself. I—*oh.* I forgot. This one's new."

"Nice try," Ryan says. "But we have your old one." He pulls it out of his interior pocket and opens the texting app and the burner app.

"You texted Jamie from the primary phone number. You texted me from a virtual number."

She nods. "Yes. So? I told you. I was being careful. What's wrong?" she asks, and I turn to look at Ryan, who's scrolling through the phone.

"It's not here. The other texts between us are, but not that one. I…" He trails off and then lifts his head, looking right at her. "You could have deleted it before you tossed the phone."

"I don't even know what *it* is," she counters, but I don't think he hears her. He's working something out, and he's entirely in his own head.

It takes a moment, but he finally looks up. "Earlier today, in our texts, I called you Felicia."

She nods.

"Why didn't you correct me?"

"You texted me first. I didn't want to go off on that tangent. I just wanted to know if you were going to help me. I regretted running when I saw you. But I was unprepared then."

"You never sent any texts specifically saying you're Felicia?"

"I swear, no." Her eyes are wide. She looks completely earnest. And I hold my breath, unsure where any of this is going. "I don't know how you got that text, but—"

"It's okay," he says, looking straight at Gabby. "I do."

Chapter Seventeen

"You do?" Jamie asked, staring at him. "How?"

"Someone either cloned her phone or is spoofing a number. Wouldn't be too hard."

"Really?" Gabby said, her nose wrinkled in disgust. "I figured you could track me—because of your job, I mean—but I never thought of that. You honestly think so?"

"If someone is trying to hurt you, I think you're always better off assuming that they have a lot of resources. You've been lucky."

"But here's the real question," Jamie said. *"Why?"*

Gabby shrugged. "I wish I knew, and God knows I've thought about it nine ways from Sunday because once I knew someone was trying to kill me, I was desperate to figure out why. I mean, hey. I read a lot of mystery novels."

Jamie pointed at her. "And *that* is the Gabby I remember. Smarts mixed with a dash of snark."

"I haven't been feeling too snarky lately. But I knew that Randall was worth a fortune, and I knew that money makes people crazy. But money would be a stupid motive, because I didn't inherit anything. Believe me, I would know if I was suddenly swimming in millions."

"Any other motives come to mind?" Ryan asked.

She looked at him—straight at him—and then nodded. "Yeah. And I'm sorry about this one. It's probably crazy and I don't mean to bring back memories, but I wondered if someone from the past thinks I'm Felicia—and is annoyed because she's supposed to be dead. Crazy, I know, but I also read a lot of thrillers."

Ryan glanced sideways at Jamie, who was grinning right back.

"What?" Gabby asked.

"Not crazy," Jamie said. "Been there."

"And you ruled it out?"

Jamie opened her mouth, then closed it again. Then she raised brow, as if handing the question off to him.

"That means you *haven't* ruled it out," Gabby said.

"We mostly have," Ryan countered. "But not completely. I'm no ruling anything out completely. Not yet."

She looked between the two of them, her brow furrowed. "Was m sister a spy?"

"No," Ryan said. "At least I never thought so until I met you. Sh was a sweet girl with a sharp wit. I liked her." He smiled, remembering. " liked her a lot. For whatever that's worth."

"It's worth a lot, actually." Her voice was soft, her smile a littl watery. "Thank you."

"I don't know what we're going to find out in the long run," Ryai said. "But the woman I knew was nothing but kind."

Gabby nodded, then sighed. "It's weird. I'm not sure if I want th reason behind this to be me or her. If it's her, it probably means sh wasn't the kind of woman I'd want as my sister. But at least this migh end when whoever is hunting her realizes the mistake. If it's me, I have perpetual target on my back."

She stood and stretched. "Can I use your restroom?"

Jamie pointed it out to her, then moved from the arm of his chair t the coffee table so that she was facing him straight on.

"You believe her," she said, and it wasn't a question.

"I do."

"Good. So do I."

"Pass me her backpack."

"What?"

"I believe her," he said. "But I'm not being stupid."

"Ryan, come on. I—"

"No argument, Jamie. Someone drugged you. And if she's stayin here, I want to be certain."

She picked up the backpack and tossed it to him. "She's stayin here?"

"If we send her back to a hotel and something happens, neither on of us will forgive ourselves. That's why I'm looking." He put the backpac down beside the table. "But I'll at least do her the courtesy of asking her."

"Thanks," Jamie said, then brushed a sweet kiss over his cheek. "I love you."

"I know."

A moment later, Gabby came back, her eyes a little red, a little puffy.

"Hey," Jamie said. "It's going to be okay."

"Will it?"

"Ryan believes you."

"Yeah, but he still wants to check my stuff. Go ahead." She nodded toward the backpack. "Weird acoustics in this place."

He laughed, but he still checked. Then he handed it to her. "I had to be sure."

"It's okay. I like that you're thorough. Especially if you're on my side."

"We are," Jamie said firmly.

"I'm glad. Because whoever is doing this will just keep coming after me, right?"

"I'm afraid so," Ryan said. "And here's the bad news. I think it's you. Not Felicia. I think whatever's going on is all about you."

"Ryan!"

He reached over and squeezed Jamie's hand. "I know, but it makes the most sense."

"Why?" Gabby asked. "Why do you think that?"

"Because I've been thinking about Felicia. Really thinking about her, and really looking at you. I don't think she duped anyone. Maybe it was a fair guess before I knew you were you, but now? No. Holding on to the delusion that she's a spy…" He trailed off with a shrug.

"But—" Jamie cut herself off with a nervous glance toward Gabby.

"What?" Gabby looked between the two of them. "What's wrong?"

Jamie's brow furrowed as she looked at Ryan. "But then why did they leave you on the train? You said that supported the theory that the train attack was an extraction."

"Supported," he agreed. "But it doesn't prove anything. And the more I think about it, the more I think I was just lucky. The train was almost across the bridge and definitely over the border by then. And, hell, maybe they wanted a survivor. Someone to go back to Randall and pour salt in his wound. Maybe they were just lazy and thought I'd bleed out."

He met her eyes. "The truth is, I'll never know why I survived.

Maybe because I was meant to find you," he added, brushing his thumb over Jamie's cheek. "In the end the only thing I know for sure is that I did fail Felicia. And holding on to a cobbled-together story that she was a spy is—well, it's just a bullshit way for me to shed a little guilt."

He stood up, then shoved his hands in his pockets as he gathered his thoughts. "Maybe anybody else in the job would have failed her too, but I was the guy at the front lines, and I didn't get it done. With you, Gabby, I will get it done. That's a promise."

He turned and met Jamie's eyes. "And I keep my promises, don't I, Kitten?"

"Yeah," she said, looking at him with so much love. "You do."

"Thank you," Gabby said, wiping away a tear. "And not to put a damper on that awesome speech, but would you mind telling me how?"

* * * *

"I swear to God, I'm going to find out who the hell is behind this," Ryan told Jamie. "Even if I didn't like Gabby, I feel like I owe it to Felicia to take care of the sister she didn't know she had."

He'd just shut the door behind Baxter and Gabby. Ryan had intended to send Baxter alone to get the rolling suitcase she'd left at her hotel, but Gabby had insisted on going too.

"I'm glad you believe her," Jamie said.

"I do," he assured her. "You never doubted."

"Blind faith," Jamie said. "And I doubted a little. I just didn't like that I did." She glanced behind her at the door. "They will be okay, right?"

"They will. I have a feeling Baxter will stick close."

"And then she'll stay in the suite with us until we can figure this out."

"That is also the plan," Ryan said. They'd just finished talking about it. How Gabby would stay with them for the next few days. How Baxter and Ryan would do everything in their power to trace the threat—and eradicate it.

He'd had to call Damien, too, of course. He and Baxter had both come to London to oversee various security related issues at the London Stark Tower and at the hotel. And protecting Gabby was decidedly not on that particular Stark International agenda. Ryan hadn't expected his friend to object, and he'd been right. Both Ryan and Baxter could still oversee the work. And at the same time, hopefully, they would save an innocent woman.

"What?" he asked, noticing the way Jamie was looking at him, her head cocked as she ran her teeth over her lower lip.

"Nothing." She held out her hand, and he eyed her warily.

"What?" he repeated, and she just thrust her hand out more forcefully until he conceded and took it.

"Good man," she said, then turned and tugged him toward the balcony, then pointed to the outdoor sofa. "Sit."

"I do love a woman who knows what she wants."

"I'm very glad to hear that," she said, then stood in front of him as she slowly pulled off the T-shirt she wore. She dropped it on the tiled balcony, then grinned at him. She wasn't wearing a bra, which he knew, but seeing her now, with her jeans hugging her curves and her nipples tight and her face full of mischief and longing...well, it just about undid him.

"What are you doing, Kitten?"

"We're alone. You've had a long and stressful day and it's not even dinnertime. I thought a little de-stressing was in order."

"Is that what you thought?" he asked, stretching his arms out so they rested on the back of the sofa.

"Uh-huh," she said. But it was more than that, of course. This was about guilt. About Jamie seeing inside him and knowing what he was battling. There was no way she could fix the past, but she could give him this in the present.

And damned if he didn't love her for it.

She shimmied out of her jeans and panties, then stood there in front of him, entirely naked. There was nothing obstructing the view behind her, and he could see London laid out in front of them, the Eye rotating slowly against a stunning blue sky.

But even that view seemed shabby compared to the woman herself.

She came closer and pressed her fingertip over his lips, silently ordering him to stay quiet. Then she reached down and unfastened his slacks so she could free his already steel-hard cock. She stroked him slowly, her eyes on his, as the ever-present embers between them grew to a full-fledged blaze.

He started to speak, but she shook her head. She took her hand away, then straddled him, holding his shoulders as she moved back and forth, her slick pussy stroking his cock in a way that was taking him closer and closer to the edge.

She kept that motion up as she lifted her hands from his shoulders to her tits. She tugged on her nipples, making the hottest fucking sound while she teased and played, and he grew harder, as if that were ever possible.

And then, God help him, she slid one hand down to stroke her clit. She started slow, in time with the rocking motion of her hips. But then she moved faster, making those noises he loved and arching back as she rocked and touched in a frenzy of motion until she was bringing both of them right to the edge, so close he knew that he was going to lose it any second, and although he wanted to fuck her so damn badly, this felt incredible.

"That's it," she said. "I want you to come like this. I want to take you there." As she spoke, her hand closed over the base of his cock and with only two more strokes, he was gone. The heavens opened up, he arched back, and he exploded all over her ass and his own goddamn pants.

It was fucking bliss, especially when she dropped to her knees and licked his cock clean before looking up at him impishly. And there, naked on her knees with his come on her chin, she grinned and said "Sometimes I like to be the one in charge."

Damn, but he loved this woman.

Chapter Eighteen

As soon as Baxter and Gabby return, Hunter gets them set up in our newly expanded room. It turns out that the connecting room is one of those middle rooms for when a group wants one large suite—in the case of the penthouse, one even *larger* suite. It's huge, with a kitchen, a seating area that includes a sofa bed, and a giant table that can be used for conferences or large dinners.

Beyond that is another connecting room of the more standard variety. One living area with a king-size bed, one bathroom, and one stunning view of London.

"So this is your room," Ryan tells Gabby, indicating the bed. "And Baxter's going to camp in the middle area on the sofa bed. He'll keep you safe, I promise. And you know where Jamie and I will be."

She shoots Baxter a shy smile and murmurs thanks.

"Happy to help," he says, and it's probably my imagination, but I think he might actually be blushing.

I don't have time to explore that possibility, however, because he and Ryan are heading out to make sure that things are progressing smoothly on the Stark International side of things.

While Gabby unpacks, I take the opportunity to go upstairs. I've hardly been there at all, and it's seriously impressive. With a grand piano, an incredible bar, and a huge dining table that I imagine doubles as an elegant conference center. There's also a sunken living area with a seriously impressive media center. So impressive that I have to talk myself out of chilling with a movie.

Instead, I remember my own Hollywood goals, set myself up at the yacht-sized table, and shoot off a quick email to Carson Donnelly, the

director who's been making noises about casting me. Not an opportunit
I want to screw up, but there is also no way I'm going home until I know
that Gabby is safe and this whole mess has been cleaned up.

Since explaining this to him would take about as long as writing th
based on a true story screenplay, I just tell him it's a family emergency, bu
that I'm ready to talk by email or phone whenever he is.

Then I cross my fingers.

I also call Nikki and leave a quick update for her. After Ryan an
Baxter talked to Damien, Ryan told me it was okay to fill Nikki ir
Though I'm sure Damien's probably already done most of that. Still,
want to give her my take on the whole thing. And I promise that I'll ge
Gabby to call her as well.

Those niceties attended to, I settle into real work and pull up th
rough cut of my most recent celebrity interview. I'd already texte
Matthew to let him know in a wholly vague way that things had gotte
crazy in London. As a result, rather than look at the footage togethe
we're working separately and then comparing notes.

I go through frame by frame, making a zillion detailed notes that ar
probably going to drive the editing team crazy, but that I think will ste
the production up a notch. I'm deep in it when Gabby joins me with he
own laptop.

"I prefer paper research," she comments as she gets settled. "Bu
since I left the States in a rush, I didn't have time to gather anything
Fortunately, I've scanned or photographed almost all my research, bu
now I have to read it on my tiny screen." She points to the tablet tha
she's set up next to her laptop.

"Knock yourself out," I say, pointing to the monster TV. "Project a
your documents up there."

"Oh, good idea." She glances behind her to the bar, then turns bac
to me with a grin. "I bet it's well stocked."

"Undoubtedly."

"And don't you think it would be a shame to project my crappy j-pe
files and blurry PDFs onto such a nice screen?"

"It certainly would."

Which explains how we end up camped out in front of the televisio
with wine, popcorn, candy, and *Magic Mike* when Baxter finds us.

"Working hard or hardly working?"

"Funny man," I say, then toss a box of Junior Mints at him.

"I give this hotel five stars," Gabby announces. "There's a movie-style candy tray under the TV. It's fabulous."

Baxter chuckles, then takes a seat on the couch and opens the candy. "Pause for a sec and I'll update you."

We do, though not as eagerly as we should—it's an awesome scene, and neither one of us wants to return to reality. Still, best to know the score.

"No hit yet on the facial recognition," he says. "But the program's projecting the run will be complete by morning. Fingers crossed."

"And you put in William and his family, right?"

"Right," Baxter says. "We used several images we found online just to be dead certain. But nothing."

I meet Gabby's eyes. "Bad news for solving this, but hopefully it means your biological family isn't trying to kill you."

She clinks her wine glass against mine. "Cheers to that."

"Glad you two are taking things in stride," Baxter says to me. "But instead of eliminating, I want to find the fucker that did that to you."

"Wait," Gabby says. "Did what?" She looks between me and Baxter. "And now that I think about it, whose face are you trying to match?"

I wince, realizing that she didn't know about the man who'd come into my room.

"We don't know." Ryan's voice rises from behind me as he climbs the last few stairs. "But when we find him, it's going to take a hell of a lot of self-restraint for me not to kill him."

Gabby turns to look at Ryan. She studies him for a moment, then shifts her attention to me beside her. "Okay. Tell me."

I don't want to say anything. I'm freaked enough by what happened to me. If it had been Gabby in that bed, I don't doubt he would have increased the dosage to a lethal amount. Or just wrung her neck.

Now, though, she's looking at me with such trust and hope that I can't justify keeping anything back. Forewarned is forearmed and all that jazz. And if nothing else, she deserves to know what she's up against.

"She can handle it," Ryan says, obviously knowing exactly where my mind has wandered. He focuses on Gabby. "If you're anything like your sister, I promise you can handle more than you think."

"It's nice hearing that," Gabby says.

He nods. "I'd help you even if she wasn't, but knowing what I do about Felicia, I'm sure that this is what she'd want, too."

And it's a way to atone.

He doesn't say the last, but I'm certain it's what he's thinking. And while I hate that he thinks that he needs atonement, I'm weirdly glad that this chance—this woman—dropped into our lives.

Gabby nods slowly. "I wish I'd known her. I mean, we're identical, so maybe I do, but…" She trails off, then wipes her damp eyes. "Anyway, this isn't the point. Whose face are you matching? The person who's after me?"

"He was here," I tell her bluntly. "Or someone was. And it was probably him."

"Here?" She gestures around the room.

"In the hotel," I say, then draw in a breath. "And, well, yeah. He was in here, too. Our bedroom. Today. Earlier." I hug myself, because it's still all very fresh and fucked up. And was it just today? How is that ever possible?

"Oh my God. How?"

"He—well, Ryan was out and I was dozing, and he got in and drugged me." I'm not sure when Ryan joined us on the couch or when I moved, but I'm curled up in Ryan's lap now, his arms tight around me.

"How did he get in?"

"He cloned a maid's key. And I can assure you that will never happen again at a Stark property."

"Oh." She exhales loudly. "Wow. I'm glad you told me. And not glad all at the same time. But I'm *definitely* glad that you're helping me. Thank you."

"You're welcome," Ryan says. "But it's not just you. It's not even just Felicia. The son-of-a-bitch violated my wife. This is ours now as much as yours. Which means you have our help whether you want it or not."

"Believe me, I do. Can you show me the face? Maybe I know it."

"Of course," Ryan says.

"I've got it on my phone," Baxter says. "Hang on."

Ryan shakes his head, obviously annoyed. "Things are moving fast. We should have done that already."

"It wasn't that long ago that you had me slammed against the wall with your arm against my neck. Cut yourself some slack."

He winces, then holds out the phone that Baxter passes him. "Familiar?"

She studies it but shakes her head. "Not at all. And I'm betting the ball cap isn't helping the program."

"It slows it down," Baxter says. "But we'll get there."

Gabby meets his eyes, then looks back to me. "I like his confidence," she says, and I swear I see Baxter blush again. "Is it okay if I leave my computer stuff up here? I'll get back to it in the morning."

"Of course," Ryan says. "Are you crashing?"

She nods. "I doubt I'll sleep."

Baxter clears his throat and tells her that they can watch a movie if she needs a distraction, and because my mind always goes *there*, I have to look down at my feet and press my lips together tight in order to keep from sharing with the class the kind of distraction I think he's hoping for.

"Naughty," Ryan whispers to me as we all head downstairs moments later.

"I have no idea what you're talking about," I say primly.

We tell them goodnight, and when the connecting door closes behind him, I take my husband's hands in mine. "You think she'll be okay?" I ask. "Really?"

"We'll see that she is." He lets go of my hand to cup my cheek. "And as for tonight, Baxter has a great bedside manner. She'll be fine. Right now I want to know how you are."

I sigh as I tilt my head into the warmth of his palm. "Well, I'm better than she is. At least there's no target on my back." I frown, then look into Hunter's icy blue eyes. "Is there?"

His expression is grim. "As long as I'm helping her, you may have a bull's-eye. That sedative was just a warning."

"Oh. Great." I draw in a long breath. "Well, fortunately I look good in black and white and red. Because you can't not help her."

"And that's why I love you." His soft voice is like a caress. "You pretend like you're tough."

"Pretend." I bite my lower lip as if considering. "Yeah, pretty much."

He shakes his head, a smile dancing at the corner of his mouth. "Nope. You pretend to the world, but it's a double-blind. The truth is you are tough. A tough shell around a sweet marshmallow of a woman."

I wrinkle my nose. "Marshmallow? That's the best you've got?"

He laughs. "It's been a long day. You choose your metaphors."

I raise a shoulder. "I don't know. I just feel bad about everything that's happened to her. And it's all the worse because I like her. I always have."

"I do, too. And it is horrible. And," he adds, lifting my chin so that I'm looking him straight in the eye, "I don't like you being in the crossfire."

Warning bells clang in my ears, and I shake my head. "Oh, no. I am not leaving you now. No way."

"Jamie…"

"No," I say. "I'm safe with you. And I'm not leaving Gabby." I move closer, easing my arms around his waist. "I'm sticking, Hunter. Deal with it. Besides," I add, "I have my uses."

I press against him, feeling the way his chuckle reverberates in his chest. "Do you…?"

"Oh, most definitely. For example, you look stressed. That's no good." I slide my hands down, then cup his ass as I press my hips forward, relishing the way he hardens against me. "I'm very good at helping you relax."

"You definitely are." His hands move to cup my rear, pulling me tighter against him.

I shift, then get my hands on the button of his pants. "I think it's time for a little de-stressing."

"Kitten," he says, as I start to tug his zipper down, "I do love the way you think."

Chapter Nineteen

Ryan's dressed and almost out the door by the time I wake up.

He bends over and kisses me, and I make a sound that's not quite human. I don't do well with mornings.

"I'm going to go talk with William again," he says. "Maybe he'll be clearer today."

I force myself more awake and sit up, wishing I had an intravenous coffee drip. "Fingers crossed."

He stands in front of the full-length mirror and adjusts the tie of his slate gray suit. He looks seriously hot, and he meets my eyes in the glass and subtly shakes his head. "It's pressed. We're not wrinkling my suit."

"Spoilsport."

"Of course, William might be our bad guy," he continues without missing a beat. "Not personally—he's not doing well physically—"

"But he could be the evil mastermind," I finish.

"It's possible."

I nod. "It makes sense. Whoever spoofed her phone knew about Felicia. Enough to mention a train."

"True, but that doesn't mean much. I wasn't a secret and neither was the mission. Randall told people he was sending someone in to rescue his daughter, and I heard later that he even shared what happened to her. It wouldn't surprise me if the story went through the entire family as well as his business."

I make a face and call on the gods of sarcasm. "Well, that narrows down the suspects."

"If we just knew the endgame. Who benefits by killing her?"

"I don't know," I admit. The problem, of course, is neither does

Gabby.

He sips his coffee as he scrolls through emails on his phone presumably making sure there are no work crises before heading out on what I'm calling The Gabby Project.

"Baxter's confirmed that William's renting the house, but it looks like he's renting it from a trust called the Inheritance Trust."

"What does that mean?"

"He doesn't own the house personally, but that doesn't tell us much. There are a lot of reasons to put assets into trusts. We own a few pieces of real estate that are in a trust, actually."

"We do?"

"Well, technically I do, since I bought them before we got married." He flashes me a grin. "But I'll share if you're very, very nice to me."

I laugh. "Deal. How do you find out the reason for this trust?"

"Baxter's going to—*shit.*"

The word comes not long after a text *ping.*

"What is it?"

"Marjorie Smythe. She's dead."

"Who?"

"The attorney who handled the probate of Randall's will. Baxter says she was hit by a car yesterday. Hit and run. Her assistant told Baxter she'd try to find the specifics about the will, but it may take a while. Apparently she's new and they were moving offices. Things are chaotic."

"Oh. So...?"

"So we'll have to wait for details of the trust. Damn."

"How could a trust have anything to do with the attack on Gabby? It's all done, right? The estate is closed, or whatever they call it after everything the dead person owned is distributed. Right?"

"That's what I thought, and that's what the press about Randall's death suggests. But I was hoping Ms. Smythe could confirm."

"Maybe that private attorney you're trying to track down knows something. Or William, for that matter. If you're sure enough that he's not our bad guy that you can ask him outright."

"My gut says he's not," Ryan tells me. "He seemed to really love Felicia. Said he still imagines seeing her. That—wait."

"What?"

He starts to pace and I scoot to the foot of the bed, wanting badly to interrupt, but not wanting to disturb whatever's going on in that head of his.

"William said he adored Felicia. That he even imagined seeing her when he saw women who looked like her. And that more recently he wasn't projecting her face on other women, but actually *seeing* her. Right outside his house on the sidewalk across the street."

"Where Gabby told us she'd been."

He nods. "His wife told him that he was imagining things. She looked, too, and said that there was nobody there. And the truth is, William's a little muddled."

"But what—"

Ryan holds up a finger, silencing me. "And he said he couldn't have loved her any more if there'd been two of her."

It takes a massive effort not to say anything, but I can tell he's going somewhere with this.

Except he doesn't say anything else. Instead, he goes to the closet and flips through his suit jackets. He finds the one he wore yesterday and rummages in the pockets, coming out with a folded piece of paper. "He gave me this. A phone number for an estate agent in Somerset."

"Why?"

"I told you. He's a little muddled." He meets my eyes. "Or maybe he isn't."

I make a motion for him to hurry the hell up.

"At first, I thought maybe he was giving me the private attorney's number. But when I realized it was a dead line, I dismissed that thought and figured he was just a befuddled old man. But now I'm wondering…" He's been unfolding the paper as he talks, and I watch as his eyes go wide. "Fuck me," he whispers. "How the hell did I miss this?"

He hands me the paper, and as he starts to do something on his phone, I glance down. There's a phone number scribbled at the top—the dead one, presumably. But other than that, it's just a completed puzzle. Except, I realize, it's not.

Words fill the boxes, but don't seem to match the clues. I skim them, trying to figure out what got Ryan so juiced. Maybe a clue in the letters?

And then I see it, too. Most of the boxes are full of random words, but two answers are names. *Martin* in six-down. And *Meeks* in twenty-one across.

"The clever bastard," I whisper, and Ryan meets my eyes, then points at his phone. It's on speaker, and I hear it start to ring.

"Martin Meeks."

Oh my God, I mouth, and Ryan nods, then says, "Mr. Meeks. M
name is Ryan Hunter. I'm—"

"I know who you are, Mr. Hunter. Randall very much appreciated
everything you did for him."

"I'm happy to hear that. I'm calling about his daughter."

"Felicia."

"No. I'm calling about Gabriella."

There's a pause on the line. "Go ahead."

"Before his death, her father—well, Jeff Anderson—said she should
call you. At least, I assume it was you he meant."

"I see." Another long pause. "Is she there? Has she met with the
probate attorney yet?"

"Ms. Smythe passed away. But no. She hasn't spoken to anyone
She's—she's been laying low."

"I see," he says, and from the tone of his voice I think he doe
understand. "There are things she should know. Can I speak to her?"

I'm already off the bed by the time Ryan nods at me, and I race to
the other side of the suite and pound on the door. Baxter opens it
looking confused, and when I tell him to get Gabby, he opens the second
connecting door to the bedroom and calls for her to come out of the
bathroom. The bed, I notice, hasn't been slept in. But the sofa bed i
Baxter's part looks thoroughly rumpled.

I meet Baxter's eyes as we wait, and I watch as red creeps up hi
neck. A moment later, Gabby emerges in a bathrobe, her mouth forming
an O when she sees me.

"Like I'm going to judge," I say, then take her arm. "Come on. W
have the attorney on the phone for you."

"Oh!"

They both follow, and we meet Ryan, who's coming toward us, b
the couch. We all sit, and Ryan puts the phone on the coffee table.

"She's here," he says.

"Gabriella?" His voice is fuzzy over the speaker phone. "My name i
Martin Meeks. I'm an attorney and a friend of your father. I understand
you haven't spoken to anyone yet about the probate of Randa
Cartwright's will?"

Her brow furrows. "No. Why would I? It didn't have anything to do
with me. It's not like Randall reached out after my dad contacted him

about the DNA results. He's never had anything at all to do with me. I mean, I assume you know all that?"

"I do. Yes. As far as what you're specifically saying goes, yes."

Gabby looks at me, and I shrug. "What does that mean?" she asks.

There's a pause, then Martin clears his throat and says, "Some of what I need to tell you is public record. Some is more personal. But I'd like confirmation that you're you. I'd like to ask you some questions that Mr. Cartwright set up. Is that okay?"

She looks completely baffled. I'm not surprised. I'm baffled, too. I catch her eye and shrug. She grimaces, then nods. "Sure. I guess."

"Who was Mr. Anderson's best friend growing up?"

"Randall Cartwright."

"And who was the third member of their group of friends?"

"I—I don't know. I didn't know about any of this until right before my father died. It was sudden—a car wreck. He didn't tell me anything."

"I see. Well, this will take a bit longer, then. And the truth is that if you are Gabriella, then there's not much time left."

"For what?" I ask, unable to keep my mouth shut.

"I'm sorry. You are—?"

"Wait!" Gabriella leans closer. "Was the friend a woman?"

Martin is silent.

"I'm right, aren't I? Lorraine. Her name was Lorraine."

For a moment, there's silence, then Mr. Meeks says, "Yes, Ms. Anderson. That was her name."

"How the hell did you know that?" I ask.

"It's my middle name." She makes a face. "I hate it, but Daddy always said it was a name that was important to him. I took a shot."

"What's going on?" Ryan demands. "Ms. Anderson's life is in danger. She's answered your questions. Now answer ours."

"Immediately following Felicia's death, Randall changed his will to leave his entire estate to William, his stepbrother."

I meet Ryan's eyes. That explains why William has the house. He probably set up his own trust.

"Following that alteration in his will, Randall received word from Mr. Anderson."

"About the paternity test," Gabby says. "Daddy said he told Randall that Felicia and I were biologically his. But like I said, he never reached out to me."

"I can't speak to that. But I can tell you that once he learned about you, Randall changed his will again. His entire estate goes to his surviving issue. If no such issue presents a claim for the estate within one year, then William inherits everything."

"And in the meantime, the property is held in trust," Ryan says, in the kind of tone that suggests the pieces are firmly falling together. As for Gabby, she looks to be in shock.

"When does the year expire?" I ask.

"Ms. Anderson will need to come forward by the end of the day on Monday," Mr. Meeks says, then outlines the procedure for doing that. "Do you understand the process?"

"I think so," she says, looking at Baxter, who nods.

"Once you've officially made a claim, your identity will be verified. You were identical twins, of course. But Randall wanted to ease the fight for you if you wanted to make the claim. I have tissue samples of his stored with various Cyro organizations so that DNA can be confirmed."

"Okay." That's all Gabby says. She looks a little shell-shocked.

"I'm very happy to have heard from you," Mr. Meeks says. "And I know your father—both of them—would be pleased."

We end the call, and Gabby looks between the two of us. "Why didn't Daddy tell me this a year ago?"

"He may not have realized that the will had been changed to include any kids, and not just Felicia," Ryan says. "Or maybe he thought the estate would be an albatross. We'll probably never know."

"Maybe he only learned about the will recently," I suggest. "Around the time he started to fear someone was trying to hurt you."

"My uncle, you mean." Her voice is full of bitterness. "Maybe Daddy just knew that this was not a family I would want to be a part of."

"It's not William," Ryan says. "He's the one who snuck me this number. But I think it's time for a talk with his wife."

Chapter Twenty

The cab pulled up in front of William's home just as Ryan was ending his call. He slipped his phone into his pocket and stepped out onto the sidewalk in time to watch the front door open. The maid he remembered from his last visit stepped out with a suitcase. That was when he noticed the Rolls-Royce idling a few yards up.

"Is William available?"

She shook her head. "I'm sorry, sir. He's resting. He just took his medicine. I'm afraid he's not doing well."

Ryan glanced at the suitcase, a sense of urgency building inside him. "You're going away?"

"Yes. The family is going to the country. Mrs. Atkinson hopes the fresh air will be better for Mr. William."

"And Mrs. Atkinson. Is she available?"

"No, sir. She's packing."

"Not a problem. I'll wait in the front hall. It's important."

She gaped at him, but he turned toward the house and continued on. As Ryan knew well, acting like you had authority was often as good as actually having it.

When he reached the doorway, he turned back, pleased to see that the maid was not behind him, but had continued toward the waiting Rolls.

Good.

He entered, then went through the front hall to the library. He had no intention of waiting for Carolyn Atkinson. He needed to talk to William, and he desperately hoped the old man was still coherent.

He wanted to kick himself for not realizing it before, but until he knew about the one-year survivor clause, the bell hadn't rung. Now, though, he understood.

Carolyn Atkinson had a plan. Keep her husband alive long enough to fully inherit the estate. But keep him doped up so that he didn't spoil anything by revealing the existence of Gabby. Or, God forbid, trying to contact her.

Considering the crossword clue, William had been reasonably sharp when Ryan had been here last, but he feared that the maid had reported his visit—and that the meds had been increased. With luck, once he was off the drug, whatever it was, his faculties would return.

He assumed that as his wife, Carolyn was William's beneficiary, which meant that once the estate was vested in William, his life would be in jeopardy, too. Carolyn would simply wait a reasonable time, then increase the dose or smother him in his sleep or send him "sleepwalking" in front of a train.

And as far as Ryan was concerned, now that he'd figured that out, if he didn't prevent it, the death of Gabby's uncle—the uncle who had loved Felicia—would be on him.

Hopefully William would be coherent and able enough to leave with Ryan voluntarily. But either way, Ryan was getting the man out.

He reached the library only to have his hopes shattered. The old man sat in the same recliner, but even though barely any time had passed since Ryan's last visit, he appeared shrunken under the blanket. He smacked his lips and a stream of drool trailed from the corner of his mouth.

He looked asleep, but his eyes were wide open, staring somewhere over Ryan's head.

"William?" His voice was a whisper.

There was no response.

"William?"

Ryan stepped closer and saw the little paper cup on the floor beside him. Apparently, he'd just been dosed. And probably higher than usual in preparation for the car ride.

"Come on, sir," he said, moving forward to ease the man's dead weight out of the chair. "We're just going to get some fresh air."

William's eyes widened, and in a low, craggy voice, he murmured "Go."

"Yes. Yes, sir. We're going to go. Come on." Since there was no wheelchair, he assumed the man could walk. He bent to get an arm around him, but as he did, William grabbed his hair and shoved him down.

Not expecting the move, Ryan struggled to get his balance, only to see William snatch the heavy walking stick, and with more strength than he expected from a man in William's condition, he slashed it around in front of him, missing Ryan's head by only three or four inches.

Ryan heard a *thud*, and he turned around in time to see Carolyn Atkinson fall to the ground. In the chair, William chuckled, then looked at Ryan, his eyes still foggy, but his word surprisingly clear. "Bitch."

"Sir…how?"

William grinned, then shoved his hand into the crevice between the cushion and the arm of the chair. When he pulled it up again, his palm was full of pills. "Hid as many as I could. Would have said something that first day, but I've never been sure of Jennifer—that's the maid. And today? Well, Carolyn's been lurking. *Ah, ah, ah.*" He lifted the stick and pointed it again at the woman now struggling to get up.

"Allow me," Ryan said, taking the walking stick and pressing the capped end on her chest to hold her down.

"Mrs. Atkinson!" Jennifer called, rushing in. "There's a constable here, and—"

"Jennifer," Ryan said as the constable followed her in, "why don't you take a seat? I'm sure Constable Higgins is going to have plenty of questions for you. Constable, your timing couldn't be more perfect. I'd like to introduce you to Mr. William Atkinson. I think you'll be interested in what he has to say."

"I'm sure I will, sir," Higgins said as another constable and a sergeant arrived while Carolyn Atkinson went white with fury.

"The chief inspector's outside, sir," Higgins said.

"I'll go see him," Ryan said, then patted William's shoulder. "You're in good hands. I'll be back soon. And then there's someone I want you to meet."

He left William with the constable, then headed out, thankful that he'd been right, that William was now safe, and that the hunch behind his call to Higgins—who he knew well since the constable's beat included the London Stark Tower—hadn't turned out to be completely wrong.

He waved to Chief Inspector Gregson, then held up a finger as his phone rang, showing Baxter's caller ID.

"He's here," Baxter said, his voice strong with victory. "The son-of-a-bitch is right here in the goddamn building."

Ryan met Gregson's eyes, and the two men headed for the chief inspector's car. "Hold him," Ryan ordered. "I'm on my way."

Chapter Twenty-One

"He's here," Baxter says into the phone, his voice strong with victory and his eyes wide with the thrill of the chase. "The son-of-a-bitch is right here in the goddamn building." He listens, then nods. "Will do." A beat, then he looks at me and nods. "Ryan's on his way."

"Thank goodness," I say, sitting down at the polished table, my coffee mug warm in my hands.

"Who's here?" Gabby asks. She's leaning in the doorway, freshly showered and now in shorts and a tank top. I notice that Baxter is working very hard not to look in her direction. "Sorry I took forever. I needed a long, hot shower."

I glance toward Baxter and lift my brows. "Some kinks to work out?"

Her mouth twitches. "A few," she says, then breaks into a wide grin.

Baxter, who now has his back to me, turns. "What?" he asks, but I can only wave the question away as Gabby repeats, "Who's here?"

"The son-of-a-bitch who drugged Jamie," Bax says, meeting my eyes as a tremor cuts through me. I want him caught, but I don't like the idea of being anywhere near that guy. And even the top floor of the hotel seems too close to the lobby.

"That's great, right?" Gabby asks. "You can detain him and call the cops and then we figure out who he is."

"And who he's working for," I say. "Although it's got to be Carolyn Atkinson, right? Did Ryan say what happened at the townhouse?"

Baxter shakes his head. "But he's on his way. He'll fill us in when he gets here. In the meantime, hang on." He scrolls through his phone where I know he's getting constant text and voice updates from the hotel security team.

"Ryan's with the chief inspector. A team is at the townhouse. Carolyn's in custody. William is under medical care." He looks up from the screen. "Now you're updated."

"I can't believe this is almost over," Gabby says. She has her own cup of coffee now, and she takes a long sip, then sighs.

"We grab the bastard," Baxter says. "He'll confirm that Carolyn hired him—or maybe blackmailed him—to drug Jamie and probably go after Gabby. And then we can wrap this up."

"That would be amazing," Gabby says. "But are we absolutely sure this is the guy? Because why would he come back?"

"He must not know that we have his picture or even that we've been looking for him. Which means we have the upper hand." I look to Baxter. "Right?"

He nods, then moves to Gabby's side. "And he damn sure doesn't know that we've had multiple agents stationed at all of the monitors in the security room watching to see if he returned to the hotel."

"But that still doesn't explain why he'd come back at all," she asks.

Baxter meets her eyes. "You heard what Meeks said about the will. They're running out of time."

"Oh, God." The blood drains from her face. "Of course. He's here for me."

"He won't get you." I'm adamant.

"No," Baxter agrees. "He won't. He's probably planning to watch the room. See when you leave to go shopping, down to the spa, whatever. Then he'll make his move, grab you, and Bob's your uncle."

She actually laughs. "You don't sound remotely British."

He shrugs. "Which is why I work for her husband instead of making a living on the BBC." He hooks a finger my direction, then smiles.

His phone pings, and he glances down, then back up again. "And it's time."

"Time?" I ask, then answer myself. "You have his location in the hotel and you're going to go get him?"

"Already got him," Baxter says. "Ryan pulled the trigger on the team intercepting him when we started this conversation. Our mysterious infiltrator is waiting in Ryan's office. Hang on."

Gabby and I watch as he crosses the room to make a quick call. "They picked him up for loitering," he says, returning. "Said some women complained that he was hitting on them, and we don't believe he's registered at the hotel."

"That's perfect," I tell him.

"He's locked up and Carolyn is in custody. Ryan's on his way in. We should have this tied up with a bow within the hour." He points to each of us in turn. "Stay put, though. I'm heading down to start talking with our guy."

We agree, and as soon as he's out the door, I flip the security lock. "I need a drink. You?"

"God, yes," she says, then follows me to the bar.

I grab a package of chocolate chip cookies from the hotel's welcome basket, noticing that Ryan left his personal phone beside it. I roll my eyes. He knows every minute of every day where his work phone is, but I find his personal one all over our house. He keeps telling me he's going to combine both numbers on one device but hasn't gotten around to it yet.

I toss Gabby the cookies, and she catches the package one handed. Then I pour us each a Scotch and follow her to the sofa where we each take a corner, both of us curling one leg up so that we probably look like bookends.

"So what now?" she asks.

"Ryan's good at getting information," I tell her. "He'll drag it out of this dude, find out if anyone else is involved, and then nail Carolyn and anyone else's ass to the wall. And somewhere in there they'll get local law enforcement and the embassy involved, too, I'm sure."

"Right. So, how long will that take?"

I shrug. "Fifteen minutes? An hour? More? It all depends on the willpower of the man in the chair."

She shoots me a pained look, and I grimace. "I know. Waiting is the worst. Should we, I don't know, watch a movie?"

Gabby laughs. A real, genuine, stress-relieving laugh. "That's normal," she says. "And right now, normal sounds very, very good." She grabs the remote from the coffee table and clicks to one of the streaming services. We're about twenty minutes into *Pitch Perfect* when my phone pings, and she pauses the film.

It's a text from Ryan, and it says—*Progress report: All good. We're wrapping up. Stay in the room. Back soon. Love you.*

I put my phone down, but before she starts the movie again, Gabby looks at me. "Do you know the worst? I don't even care about the money. I mean, Carolyn is my aunt, right? Why do all of this? We could have spl it. I might have even told William to take most of it—I probably would have. I didn't know Randall, and I'm fine financially. I mean, hindsight is twenty-twenty, but all I want is something from Randall that commemorates the fact that he thought about me. Like a memento, or even a few shares of stock in his company, you know?"

"I get it," I tell her. "Do you even know what kind of business Randall was in?" It occurs to me that Jeff might not have had the chance to tell her how her birth father made his fortune. A fortune she's going to inherit.

"I looked it up on the flight over. All sorts of tech stuff, but most recently the company was focused on cellular technology. Mobile phones and that kind of thing."

I nod. "Yeah, that's what Ryan told me. Weapons and communications." I glance at my own phone, then frown.

"What?"

"I'm not sure. Something…" I trail off, then shrug. "One of those thoughts you can't quite catch."

She looks at me expectantly as I sit there, but then I shake my head again and make a frustrated noise.

"Whatever it is, you'll remember when you're not trying." She clicks the remote to start the movie again.

We're almost to the big finale when I hear the distinctive click of a key card at a hotel door. I glance toward our door but see no telltale light and no movement of the doorknob. The click, I realize, isn't coming from this room.

Baxter.

He must be back already, and since he has a key to both the connecting conference room and Gabby's room beyond that, he must be coming in through one of those entrances. I get up, already expecting him to holler for us when the security latch engages, preventing the door from opening more than a few inches. But then I remember that although I latched the penthouse door, neither Gabby nor I thought to go into the connecting rooms.

Baxter doesn't need me to unlatch the door, but I continue that direction anyway, hoping Ryan's with him. I'm halfway to the conference room when I stop dead in my tracks.

Ryan's text to me came in with the label Husband.

That's the way I have his personal number in my contacts. It started as a joke, and I ended up keeping it. His work number is labeled Hunter.

Which means that the text telling me and Gabby to stay put came from Ryan's personal phone. But his personal phone is by the hospitality basket at the bar.

I remember Gabby's cloned and spoofed phone. And now Ryan's been spoofed, too.

And, gee, Randall's company deals in cellular tech.

Fuck.

I turn to Gabby, my heart pounding, and before she can ask what the problem is, I put my finger over my lips. Then I hold out my hand and signal for her to come to me quietly.

Her eyes widen with fear, but she complies, and as soon as she reaches me, I grab her hand and aim us both for the door.

She's with the program now, and we hurry silently the rest of the way. I fumble for the security lock, wishing I'd thought to turn the movie back on because the a cappella singing would mask the sound.

I've just managed to get the latch free and am about to pull the door open when I hear the slightest *tap* from behind me. I don't know what it is—a footstep, maybe?—but instinct kicks in and I lunge toward Gabby, knocking her sideways as a shot rings out. My head goes numb and my ears are ringing, but I still hear Gabby's scream, mingling with the ocean deep roar in my ears.

At the same time, I see blood on the wall beside the door and hear my own scream fill the room.

I whip my head around to see Gabby. She's still standing, but she seems to be heading toward the floor. I help the process by grabbing her and tugging her down toward the tile. In the process, I realize that the blood is coming from her upper arm.

Terror rips through me, but in that infinitesimal moment, I note that her arm isn't spurting and figure that must be good. Surely that means an artery wasn't hit, right? And maybe my leap onto her kept the bullet from hitting her chest.

Everything is happening in slow motion, like a split second of time in a movie. Then time returns to normal as we hit the ground hard, and I roll on top of her whimpering, limp body.

Shock, I think. *We're both in shock.*

At least I know that the bullet didn't kill her. And since our assailant was only a few yards across the room and our backs were turned before heard the footstep, I think that he must not be a professional criminal.

And that's when I know. That's when it all clicks.

Patrick. William's son. A doctor who could supply drugs for me and for William. A kid who would have grown up around his tech-savvy uncle.

He was about to be ousted in favor of a cousin he'd never even met. And he—and his mother—were pissed.

I lift my head, and my rapid-fire thoughts are confirmed when I see the face of a man I'd seen only once in a photograph.

The world is hazy as I try to push myself up. My ears are still ringing. I'm terrified, my insides shaking in a way that I can't seem to turn off. But the thing that's foremost in my mind? It's that unlike in the movies, this guy shot first, without laying out his nefarious plan so that we would know what he was up to.

But now, I realize he's going to do it again, and there is no way in hell that I can outrun a bullet. I see him raise the gun. I see him sneer. And then I see nothing at all because I throw myself back down, my body covering Gabby's, as if I'm some sort of magic armor that can save both of us from the power of a bullet.

I brace myself—and then I hear the shot.

I flinch, expecting ravaging pain, maybe even darkness, and my mind fills with Ryan and regret, because how can I go without saying good-bye?

But there is no pain. Instead, there's the whiz of a bullet. Close—so terrifyingly close—and a harsh *crack.* It takes me a moment before I realize that the bullet arrowed through drywall and embedded in the stud.

I look over and see Ryan falling to the ground, Patrick beneath him with the gun extended.

They hit the floor and another shot rings out, and I'm sure it's the end. But it's not.

There's no pain. No more sounds. There's nothing except the ringing in my ears and then—as if underwater—I hear my name.

"Jamie. Jamie. Jamie."

I want to move, but I can't. What if it's a trap? What if Patrick wants me to be facing him when he kills me? What if he wants to put a bullet through my head, clearing the way for him to drag Gabby out of here and do horrible things to her?

What if Patrick is the last person I see alive?

I don't think I could stand that.

And then I hear the sweetest sound in the world. I hear Ryan's voice saying, "Kitten." And in that moment I realize how I had been so stupid earlier. Because there was no way he would have said simply *Love you* in that text. My Ryan would have said *Love you, Kitten.*

* * * *

I must have passed out, because I wake in darkness hearing random noises. Rustling. Voices. Movement.

"Open your eyes, Kitten."

Relief floods my body, and I force my eyes open to find Ryan smiling down at me. There's another face, too. A ruddy-faced ginger-haired man who's holding my arm, which is wrapped in a blood pressure cuff.

"You're okay," Ryan says as the redhead nods his agreement and removes the cuff. "It's over."

"I passed out?"

"I can't blame you. That bullet embedded in the wall missed your head by a fraction of an inch."

My stomach rolls, but I hold it together. "What about Gabby?"

"She'll be fine. Paramedics took her to the hospital, just to make sure Baxter went with her. But she only had a flesh wound. They'll keep her overnight for observation, and my guys and the London cops are keeping an eye on her. But that's just overkill," he adds, probably in response to my alarmed expression. "Patrick's dead, and we have Carolyn and the guy they hired in custody, telling everything he knows. Name's John, and he's got a rap sheet a mile long. Says he was blackmailed into doing Patrick's dirty work. Patrick gave him the drug, but John's the one who broke in and injected you."

"That's why the facial recognition didn't find Patrick."

Ryan nods. "And why he came back—this time *with* Patrick. They're almost out of time and must have been panicking. And they didn't know if we'd ID'd their guy, but Patrick went with him just in case. When we caught John downstairs, Patrick took over. He wore a hat, dark glasses, and kept his head down."

"What about Carolyn?"

"Local authorities have her in custody. She says her son threatened her and was out of control. I don't believe it, and neither do the locals. We're ninety-nine percent sure it was just the two of them—plus John—but we'll firm up that last one percent."

"And Baxter? He's okay?"

Ryan nods. "He was right behind me when I rushed Patrick. He got to you before I did."

"I'm glad he's safe."

"And I'm glad you are. Christ, Kitten, if—" He shakes his head. "No ifs. You're alive, and you'll be fine."

"We both will," I say, squeezing his hand.

"What exactly happened? Gabby was in no condition to talk before they took her away."

I tell him the story, including the part about realizing he hadn't sent the text.

He cringes. "That does it. One phone, both numbers. By the end of the day."

I shake my head. "Tomorrow's soon enough. You won't need to text me today. You're not leaving my side."

"No," he says. "I'm definitely not."

I realize that everyone who had been in the room has left, and it's just me and Ryan in the bedroom. And the moment I realize we're alone, the dam breaks. A huge sob forces its way up my throat, and with a shudder, I wrap my arms around my husband and cling to him. "I was horribly scared," I whisper.

"I know," he says, stroking my hair. "God, Kitten, I know."

I feel the tension in him, and I know what it means. I let him hold me a while longer, but then I have to pull back. I have to see his eyes. And he has to see mine. "It's not your fault," I say.

"Isn't it? We should have looked more deeply at Patrick."

"You looked. He was in Belgium. And he wasn't the guy who injected me. Not directly."

He ignores me. "I should have had armed guards at your doors."

"Dammit, Hunter, don't do this to yourself. You didn't hurt me, you saved me. If you hadn't come when you did—if you hadn't killed—"

His mouth crushes against mine, silencing me. The kiss is long and hard, and I respond instantly, my body firing with the need to prove that I'm alive. That he is, too. And that the only way to truly heal is together.

"Hunter," I murmur, breaking the kiss just long enough to breathe his name.

He doesn't answer, just eases me back onto the bed, then slowly strips off his clothes before doing the same with mine.

My body is on fire, and I want him desperately, but he teases us both with the slowness of his movements. The tenderness of his touches, the sweetness of his kisses on my lips, my jaw, my breasts, my everywhere.

I tremble beneath him, letting his ministrations wash all of the fear out of me, until every cell in my body is full of him. His love, his desire, his need. Because then there's no room for fear, only passion. Only love.

He takes me gently, his body strong over mine, as if he is protecting me even now as he claims me, and I arch up, craving that connection, needing to be *one*.

"I couldn't stand to lose you," he whispers as he moves in me.

"You can't lose me," I tell him as my soul spirals up, closer and closer. "We're two halves of a whole. Don't you know that?"

"I do," he says. "But tonight, I need a reminder."

"I'm yours," I promise him, as he leads me right to the edge. "And I'm fine. Right now, I'm more than fine." My voice trembles as I add the last, and after that I can't talk anymore. We'd been moving languidly, but now passion takes over and he claims me fiercely as I scrabble for him too, my nails digging into his back as I try to pull him into me, to finally truly be one with him.

His body shudders violently, and he cries out my name, and I feel the force of his explosion ricocheting through me with such intensity i pushes me over and I shatter in his arms until, at last, we are twined together, bodies slick with sweat, neither of us knowing where one ends and the other begins.

"I love you," he whispers. "And I will always keep you safe."

"I know," I tell him, snuggling close to this man—this miracle—m heart full of the knowledge that he is mine. And, more importantly, I am his.

Chapter Twenty-Two

One week later

"I'm going to miss you," I tell Gabby. She and Ryan and Baxter and I are sharing fries—well, *chips*—and drinking wine before Ryan and I head off to the airport. "I never thought when I started this crazy trip to seduce my husband that it would end up even crazier." I frown, then look sideways at Ryan. "Maybe I should stop that whole seduction thing. It's a bit risky."

"I eat risk for breakfast," he says, stealing a fry off my plate. "And considering I've gained a sister-in-law, I have no regrets." He and Gabby share a smile, and I know they're both thinking of Felicia. The sister she never knew. The wife he never really had.

After a moment, she draws in a satisfied breath, then reaches for both our hands as she smiles at Baxter, across from her. "Seriously, you guys—I was in hell when I came here. My father—the only father I knew—had just died, and under pretty scary circumstances. And then suddenly I was running—or rather, hiding—for my life."

I squeeze her hand. "But you're safe now."

She nods. "I know. Believe me. But I still don't get why Carolyn and Patrick waited so long. I mean, why not kill me the moment they knew about the survivor period?"

"That's part of why I wanted to see you today," Ryan says. "Other than just saying good-bye, I mean."

"We talked to William yesterday," Baxter adds. "Carolyn didn't know about you at first."

Gabby takes another french fry as Ryan explains. "Apparently, your Uncle William got in touch with Jeff after Randall's death. But Jeff was angry with Randall for never reaching out to you. Even so, he told William that he'd talk to you, and the decision about whether to make a claim would be yours."

Gabby shakes her head. "He never told me. But about a year ago we did talk about what it would be like to win the lottery. It was a very strange conversation, actually, and I told him I thought it could end up being more of a curse than most people anticipate."

"Maybe that's how he justified the decision," Baxter says. "Because somewhere he decided not to tell you."

"But he changed his mind," Gabby says, looking between Ryan and Baxter. "Do you know why?"

Ryan nods. "William called Jeff a few weeks ago and told him to reconsider. He said that Randall may have pulled away, but that he—that is, William—wanted a relationship, and that it had to start honestly." He takes a sip of water. "But William was also ill at the time and on meds. He told me that after the conversation he got fuzzier, his health and mental acuity starting to fade."

"They'd altered his meds," I say.

Ryan nods. "Turns out that Carolyn hadn't known about Gabby before, but she overheard the conversation. And about the time that Jeff was prepared to tell you, Carolyn and Patrick set the wheels in motion to take you out of the equation altogether."

"Wow," Gabby says. "It's only luck that I survived the car wreck. And over here, you saved me. Literally. And I won't ever forget it."

"You won't be able to forget it if I have anything to say about it," I say.

Her forehead creases. "What do you mean?"

"I had a conference call with Matthew Holt last night. He totally wants to option the rights to your story. Yours too," I say, pointing to Ryan. "And guess who's going to work with him to produce? And maybe—fingers crossed—even star."

"That's great," Gabby says, laughing. "Weird, but great."

"You sure you don't want to come back to the States and meet him? See Nikki? She's dying to hear about all this firsthand."

"I've seen the articles about her and Damien," Gabby retorts. "She can get to London easily enough if she wants to."

"True," I concede.

"And I want to stay here for a while and get settled. Hang out," she adds with a glance toward Baxter. "And I want to get to know my uncle."

Gabby's moving in with William, and Mr. Meeks is handling the consensual change in ownership, making them joint owners of all the property Gabby's now inherited.

"He's looking forward to it," Ryan says. "He's especially glad to have you with him, all things considered."

Gabby nods, and I know we're all thinking the same thing. It's been hard on William knowing that his wife and son both conspired to try to kill Gabby, and in the process tried to keep William drugged up and out of commission. Having Gabby there can't erase that pain, but it will help.

Patrick is dead now, of course, but Carolyn and the flunky who dosed me are alive and in custody, buried under the weight of many charges, including the conspiracy to kill Marjorie Smythe. The accident had been no accident.

"You okay?" Ryan asks, leaning close and lowering his voice.

"Just melancholy. I'm happy to be going home, but I feel like I'm leaving Gabby all over again."

"This time won't be like school," he assures me, then grins. "You two are family now."

"Yeah," I say, leaning in as his arm tightens around my shoulder. "Speaking of family, I was thinking. Even though we don't have to get married again, what would you think about having a second honeymoon? It's a long flight home, and a mile-high honeymoon sounds pretty good to me."

"Kitten, I think that's a marvelous idea."

* * * *

Also from 1001 Dark Nights and J. Kenner, discover Cherish Me, Indulge Me, Damien, Hold Me, Tame Me, Tempt Me, Justify Me, Caress of Darkness, Caress of Pleasure, and Rising Storm.

* * * *

Charismatic. Dangerous. Sexy as hell. Meet the elite team at Stark Security.

Shattered With You
Broken With You
Ruined With You
Wrecked With You
And more to come...

Sign up for the 1001 Dark Nights Newsletter
and be entered to win a Tiffany Lock necklace.

There's a contest every quarter!

Go to www.1001DarkNights.com to subscribe.

As a bonus, all subscribers can download
FIVE FREE exclusive books!

Discover 1001 Dark Nights Collection Seven

THE BISHOP by Skye Warren
A Tanglewood Novella

TAKEN WITH YOU by Carrie Ann Ryan
A Fractured Connections Novella

DRAGON LOST by Donna Grant
A Dark Kings Novella

SEXY LOVE by Carly Phillips
A Sexy Series Novella

PROVOKE by Rachel Van Dyken
A Seaside Pictures Novella

RAFE by Sawyer Bennett
An Arizona Vengeance Novella

THE NAUGHTY PRINCESS by Claire Contreras
A Sexy Royals Novella

THE GRAVEYARD SHIFT by Darynda Jones
A Charley Davidson Novella

CHARMED by Lexi Blake
A Masters and Mercenaries Novella

SACRIFICE OF DARKNESS by Alexandra Ivy
A Guardians of Eternity Novella

THE QUEEN by Jen Armentrout
A Wicked Novella

BEGIN AGAIN by Jennifer Probst
A Stay Novella

VIXEN by Rebecca Zanetti
A Dark Protectors/Rebels Novella

SLASH by Laurelin Paige
A Slay Series Novella

THE DEAD HEAT OF SUMMER by Heather Graham
A Krewe of Hunters Novella

WILD FIRE by Kristen Ashley
A Chaos Novella

MORE THAN PROTECT YOU by Shayla Black
A More Than Words Novella

LOVE SONG by Kylie Scott
A Stage Dive Novella

CHERISH ME by J. Kenner
A Stark Ever After Novella

SHINE WITH ME by Kristen Proby
A With Me in Seattle Novella

And new from Blue Box Press:

TEASE ME by J. Kenner
A Stark International Novel

Discover More J. Kenner

Cherish Me: A Stark Ever After Novella
Coming November 3, 2020

My life with Damien has always been magical, and never more s
than during the holidays, a time for us to celebrate the hardships we'v
overcome and the incredible gift that is our family. Over the years, he ha
both protected and cherished me. He has made my life more rich and fu
than I could ever have imagined.

This year, he's treating me and our daughters to a holiday i
Manhattan. With parades and ice skating, toy displays and candies. An
most of all, with each other.

It's a wonderful gift, a trip I will always cherish. But this year, I'm th
one with the surprise. And I can't wait to see the look of delight and aw
when I finally share my secret with Damien.

* * * *

Indulge Me: A Stark Ever After Novella

Despite everything I have suffered, I never truly understood darkne
until my family was in danger. Those desperate hours came close t
breaking both Damien and me, but together we found the strength t
survive and hold our family together.

Even so, my wounds are deep and wispy shadows still linger. Bu
Damien is my rock. My hero against the dark and violence.

When dark memories threaten to consume me, he whisks me awa
knowing that in order to conquer my fears he must take control. Deman
my submission. Claim me completely. Because if I am going to find m
center again, I must hold tight to Damien and draw deep from th
wellspring of our shared passion.

* * * *

Damien: A Stark Novel

I am Damien Stark. From the outside, I have a perfect life. A billionaire with a beautiful family. But if you could see inside my head, you'd know I'm as f-ed up as a person can be. Now more than ever.

I'm driven, relentless, and successful, but all of that means nothing without my wife and daughters. They're my entire world, and I failed them. Now I can barely look at them without drowning in an abyss of self-recrimination.

Only one thing keeps me sane—losing myself in my wife's silken caresses where I can pour all my pain into the one thing I know I can give her. Pleasure.

But the threats against my family are real, and I won't let anything happen to them ever again. I'll do whatever it takes to keep them safe—pay any price, embrace any darkness. They are mine.

I am Damien Stark. Do you want to see inside my head? Careful what you wish for.

* * * *

Hold Me: A Stark Ever After Novella

My life with Damien has never been fuller. Every day is a miracle, and every night I lose myself in the oasis of his arms.

But there are new challenges, too. Our families. Our careers. And new responsibilities that test us with unrelenting, unexpected trials.

I know we will survive—we have to. Because I cannot live without Damien by my side. But sometimes the darkness seems overwhelming, and I am terrified that the day will come when Damien cannot bring the light. And I will have to find the strength inside myself to find my way back into his arms.

* * * *

Justify Me: A Stark International Security/Masters and Mercenaries Novella

McKay-Taggart operative Riley Blade has no intention of returning to Los Angeles after his brief stint as a consultant on mega-star Lyle Tarpin's latest action flick. Not even for Natasha Black, Tarpin's sexy personal assistant who'd gotten under his skin. Why would he, when Tasha made it absolutely clear that—attraction or not—she wasn't interested in a fling, much less a relationship.

But when Riley learns that someone is stalking her, he races to her side. Determined to not only protect her, but to convince her that—no matter what has hurt her in the past—he's not only going to fight for her, he's going to win her heart. Forever.

* * * *

Tame Me: A Stark International Security Novella

Aspiring actress Jamie Archer is on the run. From herself. From her wild child ways. From the screwed up life that she left behind in Los Angeles. And, most of all, from Ryan Hunter—the first man who has the potential to break through her defenses to see the dark fears and secrets she hides.

Stark International Security Chief Ryan Hunter knows only one thing for sure—he wants Jamie. Wants to hold her, make love to her, possess her, and claim her. Wants to do whatever it takes to make her his.

But after one night of bliss, Jamie bolts. And now it's up to Ryan to not only bring her back, but to convince her that she's running away from the best thing that ever happened to her--him.

* * * *

Tempt Me: A Stark International Security Novella

Sometimes passion has a price…

When sexy Stark Security Chief Ryan Hunter whisks his girlfriend Jamie Archer away for a passionate, romance-filled weekend so he can finally pop the question, he's certain that the answer will be a nthusiastic yes. So when Jamie tries to avoid the conversation, hiding her ears of commitment and change under a blanket of wild sensuality and ecadent playtime in bed, Ryan is more determined than ever to convince amie that they belong together.

Knowing there's no halfway with this woman, Ryan gives her an ltimatum – marry him or walk away. Now Jamie is forced to face her eepest insecurities or risk destroying the best thing in her life. And it will ke all of her strength, and all of Ryan's love, to keep her right where she elongs…

* * * *

Caress of Darkness: A Dark Pleasures Novella

From the first moment I saw him, I knew that Rainer Engel was like o other man. Dangerously sexy and darkly mysterious, he both enticed ne and terrified me.

I wanted to run–to fight against the heat that was building between s–but there was nowhere to go. I needed his help as much as I needed is touch. And so help me, I knew that I would do anything he asked in rder to have both.

But even as our passion burned hot, the secrets in Raine's past ached out to destroy us … and we would both have to make the reatest sacrifice to find a love that would last forever.

Don't miss the next novellas in the Dark Pleasures series!
Find Me in Darkness, Find Me in Pleasure, Find Me in Passion, aress of Pleasure…

* * * *

Storm, Texas.

Where passion runs hot, desire runs deep, and secrets have the power) destroy…

Nestled among rolling hills and painted with vibrant wildflowers, the ucolic town of Storm, Texas, seems like nothing short of perfection.

But there are secrets beneath the facade. Dark secrets. Powerful secrets. The kind that can destroy lives and tear families apart. The kin that can cut through a town like a tempest, leaving jealousy an destruction in its wake, along with shattered hopes and broken dream All it takes is one little thing to shatter that polish.

Rising Storm is a series conceived by Julie Kenner and Dee Davis t read like an on-going drama. Set in a small Texas town, Rising Storm i full of scandal, deceit, romance, passion, and secrets. Lots of secrets.

About J. Kenner

J. Kenner (aka Julie Kenner) is the *New York Times*, *USA Today*, *Publishers Weekly*, *Wall Street Journal* and #1 International bestselling author of over one-hundred novels, novellas and short stories in a variety of genres.

JK has been praised by *Publishers Weekly* as an author with a "flair for dialogue and eccentric characterizations" and by *RT Bookclub* for having "cornered the market on sinfully attractive, dominant antiheroes and the women who swoon for them." A six-time finalist for Romance Writers of America's prestigious RITA award, JK took home the first RITA trophy awarded in the category of erotic romance in 2014 for her novel, *Claim Me* (book 2 of her Stark Saga) and in 2018 for her novel Wicked Dirty.

In her previous career as an attorney, JK worked as a lawyer in Southern California and Texas. She currently lives in Central Texas, with her husband, two daughters, and two rather spastic cats.

Visit JK online at www.jkenner.com
Subscribe to JK's Newsletter
Text JKenner to 21000 to subscribe to JK's text alerts
Twitter
Instagram
Facebook Page
Facebook Fan Group

On Behalf of 1001 Dark Nights,

Liz Berry, M.J. Rose, and Jillian Stein would like to thank ~

Steve Berry
Doug Scofield
Benjamin Stein
Kim Guidroz
InkSlinger PR
Dan Slater
Asha Hossain
Chris Graham
Kasi Alexander
Jessica Johns
Dylan Stockton
Richard Blake
and Simon Lipskar

CPSIA information can be obtained
at www.ICGtesting.com
Printed in the USA
BVHW030343300420
578925BV00001B/12

9 781951 8120